India Watson is an avid reader, regular writer and sometimes adrenaline junkie. A graduate in psychology, she lives in Shropshire with her family and animals and focuses her spare time on walking and writing. She enjoys dark humour, quirky plots, and ragtag groups in found families. *#vampireproblems* is her debut novel.

To my favourite family member; you know who you are.

India Watson

#VAMPIREPROBLEMS

Happy reading

[handwritten smiley face with vampire fangs]

[signature]

AUSTIN MACAULEY PUBLISHERS™

LONDON * CAMBRIDGE * NEW YORK * SHARJAH

This is a work of fiction. Names, characters, businesses, places, events, locales, and incidents are either the products of the author's imagination or used in a fictitious manner. Any resemblance to actual persons, living or dead, or actual events is purely coincidental.

A CIP catalogue record for this title is available from the British Library.

ISBN 9781528946568 (Paperback)
ISBN 9781528971829 (ePub e-book)

www.austinmacauley.com

First Published (2021)
Austin Macauley Publishers Ltd
25 Canada Square
Canary Wharf
London
E14 5LQ

I want to thank my family: Derrick, Dawn, Debs, Mark, Holly, Jamie, Fleur, Jessica, Angus, Isabel, Stella and Margot. I would have put you all in the dedication but there wasn't enough room. Thank you all for listening to my long rambles about the plot—or pretending to listen very well—and answering my random questions like, what would happen if you put a werewolf on the moon?

I want to thank Austin Macauley Publishers for taking a chance on a new author, all the editors that helped make this into a coherent story and everyone who had a hand in making this book.

I want to thank the founders of National Novel Writing Month for motivating me to sit down and write this story, the Liverpool Writers Group I was a part of, and in particular my friend, Sian, who has been with me through all the ups and downs of writing, and was the first person to read this story, which was sort of like handing over my first born. I would also like to apologise to all of my lecturers at university, as I wrote most of this during your lectures.

Chapter One

The reveal of the supernatural community had been mostly accidental and, like most catastrophes in the world, could be traced back to one idiot who felt he could speak on behalf of people he most certainly couldn't. The idiot in this instance was named Dave and lasted about as well as you would imagine anyone could after dragging a bunch of pissed off creatures-of-the-night out of the metaphoric supernatural closet.

After the reveal, and subsequent mysterious disappearance of Dave, the world recoiled in collective horror. Politicians and world leaders quickly plastered on a smile, and with little grace or dignity, 'welcomed' the supernatural with gritted smiles and open arms that felt akin to walking into the comforting grasp of a boa constrictor.

Humans, in their infinite need to explain everything away with science, got to work on developing theories almost immediately. Most scientists eventually and uneasily settled into believing gene mutations created vampires, and werewolves by a test tube happy mad man who dabbled in gene splicing. By this point, most had retired anyway in a dramatic show of hand waving and hysterical laughter, which left all the too-young-to-give-up-just-yet scientists to sigh and say, 'Sure, why not?'

Although their scientific explanations wavered somewhat when witches came out of the woodworks, and they were forced to accept, or at least studiously ignore, the reality of magic. A few persistent scientists insisted if magic was inherited, there had to be a gene, and they clung to their logic and theories.

When scientists were finally faced with the prospect of demons, they collectively lost their shit, scientifically speaking. They hung up their lab coats and descended into debate with philosophers.

Although demons themselves would often state they were merely supernatural entities that happened to embody living beings in a similar way to what humans described as 'demons' and 'possession', their existence did not make Heaven and Hell real, in the same way that the existence of witches did not make Hogwarts real. Although this speech was often lost to the background noise of religious fanatics.

Harriet was now in her mid four hundreds. After the reveal had happened she had been subjected to endless questions off of desperate scientists, and gun-happy Americans. She personally thought humanity handled the reveal with uncharacteristic maturity, although her previous experience had been the Salem Witch Trials, which was a low bar to clear.

Over the years, humans and the supernatural had managed to cultivate the same relationship as estranged cousins might; you kept a weather eye on their business through your Facebook feed and made stilted, polite conversation when needed, but coped predominantly by forgetting they existed the rest of the time.

The government had initially offered a flood of legislation, which hindered more than helped, although their interests were undoubtedly more in the protection of their own. This lasted until Prime Minister Darrow was elected; later, it was speculated that he was a supernatural being himself, as he did not pass any further restrictions onto the supernatural community. He didn't explicitly help them either, but with their own asses covered and following Darrow's example, humans mostly adopted the outlook of ignore it and it might go away.

The supernatural community didn't, in fact, go away, they did however find safety in numbers and collectively spread along the border of North Wales in poked little supernatural neighbourhoods. To begin with, anyway.

Chapter Two

Most people assume that lectures in a supernatural university will involve werewolf fights breaking out over rivalling theoretical perspectives and magic users enchanting their lecturers for better grades. This is because humans view the supernatural, even at their most intelligent, as uncontrolled and immoral.

This is why humans prefer to attend separate universities; the supernaturally inclined prefer it because they don't have to deal with humans' snobby attitudes. Plus, they don't have to follow human curriculums, human history teachers do not like being told they're wrong by students, even if those students are vampires, who were actually present during said historical events.

Supernatural universities also offer night classes for vampires, something distinctly lacking in human universities. Harriet had tried to argue her case that she would literally get burnt to a crisp if she left her underground student flat during the day, but the admin had merely sent a bored reply, saying if she couldn't attend the lectures for personal reasons, then she would get an automatic fail, and they couldn't be creating a whole night class just for her.

She didn't know why she'd bothered anyway and signed up to the night classes at the local supernatural university.

She'd even managed to make it to her third year there before her lecturer got shot.

Now, this would seem contrary to the earlier point about supernatural lectures being as boring as human ones, if it were not for the fact that Harriet had been attending university for several hundred years (although she'd had to use the name Harry until the late 1870s) and never once before had a lecturer been shot. Although she supposed that was the price of immortality; statistically, everything was bound to happen eventually. She would have to start buying lottery tickets.

The day her lecturer got shot was not a miserable day, there was no ominous feeling in the air. It was an early evening lecture, the sun having barely set, and so the class was mostly full of half-asleep vampires.

There was ten of them in total, the third year, English Language night class; eight vampires, one witch who worked day shifts, and a werewolf who looked after his daughter during the day while his partner was at work. They were most of the way through the lecture when the door opened and a stranger strode in with a hood lowered over his head. He quickly pulled a gun out and shot Mr Jones in the head, before exiting just as efficiently.

There is an amazing phenomenon amongst students, both supernaturally inclined and not, that practically anything can happen in a lecture, and it can be guaranteed that past the hour mark only 10% will be paying any attention, and the rest will be asleep or daydreaming. Unfortunately for Harriet, 10% of 10 students was one, and she seemed to be the unlucky one who was paying attention when the shooting happened. The shooter had made such little noise and had been gone so quickly she would have thought she'd imagined the whole thing, if it wasn't for the small hole in the middle of Mr Jones' forehead.

"Oh no," he muttered, his soft Welsh accent making the words sound almost put out about the matter. He touched the hole in his head from his slumped position in his chair, the position he'd been forced into after the bullet propelled him backwards into it.

Harriet stared horrified at him for several moments, mind still stalling on the *got shot* aspect of the sequence of events, when she felt the girl next to her jolt, and in a sleep roughened voice ask, "Is that it? Is the lecture over?"

Harriet let out a strangled noise and figured she ought to call the police.

She should possibly wake up the rest of the students first.

*

The police arrived not long after for questioning. Unfortunately, out of the two police officers that came, one was human, which meant most of the questioning revolved around why Mr Jones was walking around the room, occasionally prodding inquisitively at his bullet hole.

"I'm a demon," Mr Jones said.

The supernatural officer, Officer Wellard, dutifully noted this down in his book, the human police officer narrowed his eyes, however.

"I see," he said, "And is this—" he gestured to Mr Jones, "This body your own, sir?"

Mr Jones' somewhat dopey smile fell from his face, and his voice turned harsh, or as harsh as a Welshman could ever sound, "Are you accusing me of possession?"

Several voices broke out at that, but Officer Wellard's rose above the rest, "It is a routine question, no offense was meant, I'm sure." Although he was glaring at his fellow officer, so Harriet figured he was being diplomatic.

"No, I'm not possessing anyone, as it's illegal."

"Can you prove this body is yours, sir?"

"Can I—? I've got a hole in my head! Can you see any brain matter, or a brain, for that matter?"

"Erm, no," the officer replied awkwardly, the hole in Mr Jones' head looked like a tunnel, as there was nothing in his head but flesh.

After possession had been made illegal, quite promptly after the reveal of demons, demons had to start fashioning their own bodies. It had been explained to Harriet that they could have mimicked human bodies exactly, down to the brain, lungs, and every little nerve ending, and inhabited these bodies, however, they would have had to feed the bodies, and wash the bodies, and let the bodies rest. Instead, they created the façade of humans, the look of them, but without any of the internal biology, they were quicker to create and you didn't need to bother with upkeep, why bother washing if you no longer sweated? The demon that had described this to Harriet had referred to the bodies disturbingly as 'fleshy puppets'.

Although this made sense now she could see straight through Mr Jones' forehead, and still read the lecture slides behind him.

"If you wouldn't mind coming with me to the station, and giving your account of the events," Officer Wellard said to Mr Jones, "Officer Sanwell here," he gestured to the still seething human officer, "Will stay here and question your students."

Great, Harriet thought, eyeing the officer as he regarded the room suspiciously, they got stuck with the human. Although it was amusing watching his lip curl in horror when Mr Jones turned to leave and revealed the massive exit hole in the back of his head.

As a group, they were mostly useless to the officer, most said they'd startled at the sound of the gun, seen Mr Jones' stumble into his chair, and by the time they'd turned, the gunman had vanished.

"He was a man, average height and broad, and he was wearing a black hoodie with the hood down," Harriet said, when the officer got to her.

Officer Sanwell raised an unimpressed eyebrow, "And how were you able to see this mysterious gunman, when no one else did?"

"I was sitting there." Harriet pointed to the desk at the front closest to the door, "I noticed the door open in my peripheral."

He asked her a few more questions but dropped it when he realised that was the extent of her description of the man.

"And why do you think it was that nobody else has heard this shot and came running? Nobody else has been in the room, have they?"

"No," Harriet replied, tempted to roll her eyes, "And it's probably because it's half nine in the evening and this is the only night class on in the English block tonight. No one else is here."

Officer Sanwell pursed his lips in annoyance, but eventually they were all released from the room but told to keep themselves available, should any more questioning be needed. It was around half ten at this point and Harriet headed straight for the coffee shop.

Being a vampire meant that she didn't need to eat or drink as regularly as humans did, or at all, technically. She had acquired a fondness for food, however, and as long as she drank some blood beforehand and got her borrowed blood pumping and digestive system functioning to some level, she would be able to digest the food.

She had also formed a friendship with the owner of the local 24-hour coffee shop near campus, or at least, mutual acceptance of each other. The owner was a grumpy werewolf, who, as far as Harriet could tell, owned the shop, but he didn't kick her out when she didn't buy anything, and let her stay until the early hours of the morning, reminding her what time sunrise was when she got caught up in work.

"You look awful," Dan said, and grabbed a blueberry muffin from the display cabinet and a packet of blood from the cooler.

"Thanks." She glared at him, but accepted the food, and handed over her money.

Friendship was definitely stretching it, but Dan was grumpy with all customers, so she didn't take it personally. Harriet suspected it was why he always worked the night shift, as the second member of night staff always rotated between three different staffers.

"My lecturer got shot," she said unprompted, she wasn't sure why; this was normally the point in their transaction when she nodded and took her seat across the café. The shooting had really rattled her, it had just happened so quickly, if Mr Jones hadn't been a demon he would have died, and died *instantly*. He would never have known anything else. His last words would have been detailing societal multilingualism.

"Really?" Dan said, as if he thought she might be having him on. She nodded, deciding to play it off a bit cooler, she didn't really like talking about personal feelings, even with Cora, who she'd been friends with since the 1800s.

"Yeah, he's a demon, though, I think he's mostly bothered about having to make a new body now."

Dan nodded, still looking at her dubiously, "I thought it was pretty easy to make one, for them."

"It is, just, he has to redo his passport and driver's license, think that's what he's annoyed about. All the paperwork."

"Ah."

Harriet wondered if she should start up a new line of conversation, before realising she couldn't be bothered, and Dan was obliged to make small talk because he was working, so it was likely that he also couldn't be bothered, so she excused herself and sat in her normal seat.

It was approaching two in the morning, and she'd powered through another muffin and a brownie, and was thinking of making a move back to her room, when she got the email from Mr Jones informing her and her class that due to him needing to reapply for his post pending paperwork and his new body, the class would be joining with the English day class, or rather, the day class would be rescheduled for the evening, and Ms Pickett would be teaching them for the foreseeable future.

She sent a quick reply, acknowledging the email and asking him if he would still be available for office hours. She had a brief moment where she wondered whether she should ask him how he was feeling, but she wasn't sure if that was like asking someone 'are you okay?' after a bereavement; she didn't know the etiquette for when someone had been shot in the head. Despite what supernatural soaps would have you believe, it just didn't happen that often.

He replied, telling her he wasn't allowed on campus in a teaching capacity until his face matched his ID, but any questions she could email to him, and for anything more complicated to go and see Ms Pickett.

Harriet had met Ms Pickett a grand total of two times, and that was far too many. She was a tall, thin woman, with her hair scrapped into a ponytail so severe that it simply screamed, I DO NOT CONDONE FUN. She reminded Harriet of the schoolmistresses from Victorian times.

Harriet dreaded her lecture the next evening and dragged her feet as much as she could without actually being late. She didn't even dare think what Ms Pickett would do if she were late.

It was her fear of Ms Pickett that led her to taking the furthest possible seat in the classroom from the front, which placed her next to Connor. Harriet's first impression of Connor was that he was strange, for as far as she could tell, he was human, which, while it wasn't against the rules for a human to attend a supernatural university, it wasn't exactly a regular occurrence. So much so that Harriet's class all stared at him when he walked through the door. Harriet also noticed his own classmates either not making eye contact with him when he was deciding where to sit, or outright glaring at him. Which was how he ended up in the seat next to Harriet, both of them sequestered in the back of the room.

"Hi, I'm Connor," he whispered excitedly, although there was a jumpy air to him that suggested he was prepared to jump and run if she told him to move seats.

Harriet pulled the corners of her lips back in a half-hearted smile and gave a little head nod in acknowledgment. Connor's smile slipped slightly, and he nodded in return. His eyes flickered towards the group of witches in his own class, and he deflated somewhat.

Harriet pursed her lips and tried to not let his sad face get to her. Cora had always insisted Harriet couldn't resist a stray, although Harriet would always shoot back that it had worked out quite well for Cora.

"I'm Harriet," she said, because she couldn't resist Cora's face back then, and she couldn't resist the small pout Connor was sporting now.

Connor gave a small grin.

A few days after she had basically adopted Cora, and effectively kidnapped her, she'd had a moment of 'What have I done?', where she'd had a meltdown and questioned why she'd let Cora's too-innocent face get to her. She had a feeling her meltdown was going to come sooner for Connor, because while she'd only befriended him, rather than kidnapped him, he wouldn't stop asking questions.

Despite the fact that Ms Pickett gave off the impression that if you talked during her lecture, she'd not hesitate to try and bring back the cane, Connor would not stop whispering to Harriet. Harriet was half convinced Ms Pickett was a vampire herself and longed for the good old days of hitting students, mostly judging on the death glares she kept giving herself and Connor.

Halfway through, he started writing frantically in his notebook, and Harriet was half convinced he'd actually started paying attention. She found out after the lecture he was simply writing all the questions he thought of into a list to ask her freely when they got out; she thought he'd go home, but he just started walking with her, he didn't even ask where they were going. Harriet figured she wasn't going to shake him, so she headed for the coffee shop.

"So, like if it's sunlight that burns you, could vampires go out on a really cloudy day? Does the strength of the sunlight have an impact, would it hurt less if it weren't a really sunny day? What if—"

"Why don't you already know this stuff?" Harriet interrupted, maybe she could pawn him off to Dan at the coffee shop and escape out the back, "You go to a university full of supernatural creatures, in fact, that's my question for you, why do you go to a supernatural uni?"

"I'm supernatural," he said, but he sounded unsure himself. Harriet actually stopped walking at that, she took in the look of him. His cheeks were flushed from walking, so he decidedly wasn't a vampire, if his incessant questioning hadn't given it away. He didn't look like a werewolf, you could never really tell, but most of them were tall, broad, and were quite hairy, even in human form. Connor was the exact opposite, wiry and while his hair was a thick quiff on top of his head, his arms were covered sparsely in hair.

"You sure about that?" He could have been a witch, but witches were a bit like vegans. If you met one and they hadn't told you in the first five minutes, they were probably lying. He wasn't a demon because Harriet had seen scrapes and small cuts on his hands, and there was a scab on his elbow.

"Well, maybe. My mum was a," he gestured vaguely, "something, and she died when I was three, but this druid was passing through my town when I was

17

ten told me I had a spark of magic and that I should pursue it." The words sounded well worn, like he'd been through this many times.

Harriet wondered how many witches had laughed at him; they were a hoity bunch, and druids weren't exactly the most reputable of magic users. They had been until their nature loving ways had collided with the flower power movement and now most of them were seen as drugged out wannabe witches.

"So, you came to a supernatural university because—"

"To find someone to teach me, or even tell me what I am." He sounded like he'd given up, although she supposed if he'd gotten to third year and not found anyone, it was unlikely he would now. She'd be feeling fed up too.

"Come on, we're going to get some food. Eating makes everyone feel better."

Connor perked up a bit, "So how exactly does vampire digestion work, there's surprisingly little information online?"

Chapter Three

Harriet and Connor settled in her normal booth. Harriet with her muffin and coffee, Connor with a double chocolate brownie and a large hot chocolate with whipped cream, Harriet wasn't sure where he put it all, given his skinny frame. Although it had the advantage of watching Dan angrily make up his order, he was muttering to himself that nobody needed that amount of sugar. Harriet had never realised someone could brandish squirty cream so menacingly.

"Is he a werewolf?" Connor asked, as soon as they sat down. He hadn't even bothered whispering it, so it could have been heard by a human, let alone a werewolf.

"Yes."

"Wow." Connor's eyes were still fixed over her shoulder, "Do you reckon he'd mind if I asked him some questions? The girl in my class got really pissed when I asked her."

Harriet smirked, half tempted to tell him to go ahead, Dan got particularly grumpy when anyone with a sunny disposition came along. However, her conscience got the better of her, "He's a bit—" she was more than aware that Dan could still hear her from across the shop, "shy," she settled on, as she didn't think 'anti-social' or 'moody' would go down too well. Werewolves already had enough stick for being aggressive or volatile, no need to add to the problem. Connor seemed the impressionable type.

"Oh." His shoulders sagged.

"But I believe you had some questions for me. I'm happy to answer them."

"Really?"

"Misinformation is the plague of our time."

"So, my question about the sun from before?"

"Right." She tried to remember what it was. "Yes, we technically can go out during the day, but you'd need to stick to shadows, no sunlight. You could go out fully covered and with an umbrella, but you'd look like a knob. It was much easier when ladies were required to cover themselves, carry parasols and wear gloves."

"So, you used to go out in sunlight?"

"Only on occasion. I once stuck my toe out in the sunlight to see what would happen, and it burnt off." Harriet had wanted to remember what if felt like to have the sun warming your skin, wanted to understand the poets when they spoke of lazy afternoons bathing in a meadow's sunlight. After her toe burned off, she'd been a bit terrified to go out again, even fully covered.

There were some vampires who took it to an extreme sport, shadow hopping. The most extreme doing it as the sun was rising, and the shadows shifted quickly. There were videos of them plastered all over YouTube. Harriet found she got heart palpitations from watching the videos, although heart palpitations for a vampire was equated to a resting heartbeat for a human.

"So, do you make a bite with your teeth and drink the blood, or do you have hollow fangs like snakes and suck it up?" Connor had gotten his notebook full of questions back out.

Harriet sighed; there was still so much misconception around even after a couple of decades.

"Neither, the gene mutation that caused all this, it's – try thinking of it more as a medical condition. It causes our gums to recede, which makes our teeth look particularly long and pointy." She grinned widely, and Connor's prey response kicked in and he flinched slightly. "But they're technically no different than your teeth. And we have toxins in our skin, that get released when they come into contact with sunlight, which is why we burn. If you think of us as humans with a medical condition, it becomes a lot easier."

"But then how do you drink blood?"

"Nowadays through blood bags that are donated," She pointed to the mug she had in front of her, "but before, we used to mostly hang around boxing rings, hospitals and morgues. If you caught them straight after they died, the blood was still okay. Although some used to just carry a knife and find people in dark alleys." Harriet pursed her lips, as if she could see it happening before her.

"So, you don't use your fangs, er, teeth at all?"

"Sometimes, as I said, we have toxins in our body, more than humans do, and different types. Some vampires reckon we have a paralytic in our spit, so they'd bite people, get saliva in wound, and then they could, erm, harvest their blood."

"With a knife?"

"Yes, although it's never been conclusively proven, different vampires might have different rates, or humans could have been so shocked to have been bitten by a rando in an alley they froze for a split second too long."

"Didn't scientists test this? I thought they did testing when supernaturals came out?" Connor asked, with all the innocence of ignorance.

"Those labs were horrific. Supernaturals picked apart like lab rats."

Humans never change throughout history, Harriet thought back to deformed babies left on hillsides, witches burned at stakes, laboratory testing by Nazis, human horror at what was different never changed, just the technology used to extract information.

Connor must have been no older than 20, he would have been born around the time that supernaturals were revealed; humans tended to gloss over the labs in their modern history. Although witches came out a few years after vampires and werewolves. Connor said his mum died when he was three, Harriet wondered if that was how she died.

She also noticed a stillness coming from the counter. Dan had been keeping himself busy at the front, while still eavesdropping. Vampires and werewolves tended to keep their biology close to the chest from humans and even each other. Harriet suddenly wondered how old Dan was; given their ability to grow facial hair from about 14, and their increased muscle mass, werewolves were notoriously difficult to age. Dan looked mid-twenties, maybe. Harriet wondered if he remembered the labs; she knew they took children into them as well.

"Oh." Connor seemed like he was still processing the fact that humans were monstrous, although even if he hadn't heard about this in modern history, how had he not learnt about it throughout all of history?

"Is this why everyone on my course doesn't like me?"

"Probably."

"Refill?" Harriet startled; she hadn't heard Dan approach. She eyed him suspiciously; he never came over to tables to ask for refills. If you wanted another drink, you had to go up to the counter and ask. It was probably their topic of conversation that had brought him over.

"No, thanks."

"Please," Connor said; he was moping now.

Dan seemed to fidget on the spot without moving. He looked decidedly uncomfortable. "I couldn't help but hear. You're human?"

"I'm sorry," Connor said, looking worried, as if he thought Dan was going to kick him out on principle.

"No, I just thought. You smelt, erm…" Harriet knew that werewolves heightened sense of smell made a lot of people uncomfortable. She herself had felt slightly annoyed when a werewolf had once told her all vampires smelled a bit like decay, and it had a metallic overtone if they'd fed recently. She'd asked what humans smelled like and he'd just responded with, 'I don't know, like humans, it's hard to describe, like vampires but without the decay and metal bit'.

"You just smelled a bit magic, was all, not like a witch," he hastened to add, as to not offend, probably, "But a bit, I don't know, magicky."

"Really?" Connor said excitedly, looking hopefully at Harriet as if to say, 'You heard it too, right?'. Harriet had a feeling she wasn't the only one who wouldn't be able to get rid of Connor now. Connor was looking at Dan like the sun shone out of his ass.

"What does magic smell like?" Harriet asked, she had never thought to ask about a magic smell.

"Electricity, or a storm." He sounded unsure. "There's like a crackle in the air. It's hard to explain." He looked at Connor, "You smell more like an electrical shortage, though."

Connor deflated.

"More like, like an electrical…" He scrunched up his face, as if he was looking for the word.

"Spark?" Harriet suggested.

Dan nodded, "Yeah." Connor looked slightly mollified now.

"What do demons smell like then?"

The answer 'like witches but stronger' should have been expected really.

"And werewolves?"

"Like dirt and the forest." Dan was closing off again, probably far out of his comfort zone anyway. Harriet supposed she could have guessed at what werewolves smelled like, mostly because any time they weren't at work was spent in the outdoors, normally the forest. And most werewolves got manual labour jobs because their increased strength made them a shoe in for the job, and it meant that they got to work outside more. Harriet was still surprised more werewolves weren't hippies.

"Sorry if I offended you. I wouldn't have asked normally, but you were talking about it." Dan said to Connor.

"That's okay, you're much nicer about me being a weird anomaly than most supernaturals, or people, for that matter."

"I'll get you another hot chocolate on the house." Dan hurried back off to the counter before Connor could say thank you.

"He didn't offend me. I didn't find that offensive. Was I meant to?" Connor whispered to Harriet, although Harriet had no doubt Dan could still hear them.

"No, well, most humans don't like being called supernatural and most supernatural don't like being mistaken as human." But nothing he said was particularly offensive in Harriet's book. She just shrugged at Connor.

"So, anyway, what happened with Mr Jones? It's going round that he got shot at by an assassin."

Harriet rolled her eyes, "He got shot, but I don't think it was an assassination attempt."

"Why?"

"Well, because you can't kill a demon, not by shooting him, at least. Now he just has a hole in his head."

"What if they didn't know he was a demon? Oh! Maybe they were sending a warning to someone?"

Harriet felt Connor was definitely one to watch bad supernatural soaps, but the weight of what had occurred struck her again with the mention of something as nefarious as assassination. Someone had tried to kill him, it hadn't seemed as chilling before because she still thought of Mr Jones when he'd been joking and trying to carry pencils in the hole in his head before the police had showed up, trying to see if anyone could throw balled up bits of paper through his head into the bin.

Someone had wanted him dead, had shot him. They would have killed him if he hadn't been a demon.

He would have been splayed out in the chair, bleeding. He wouldn't have been joking around and throwing paper.

"I wonder who wanted him dead. Mr Jones doesn't seem the type to get caught up in anything bad, but if it was someone he knew, they would have known he was a demon," Connor said.

Harriet was stumped; who the hell would try and kill a demon?

Dan cleared his throat and put down a chocolate monstrosity of a hot chocolate; it was covered in whipped cream, marshmallows and sprinkles. It didn't really fit in with the heavy vibe that was now at the table.

"Maybe," Dan said hesitantly, as if he didn't want to admit to eavesdropping again, not that he could help it. "Maybe they wanted him out of the way for a while. You said it's going to take him a while to sort paperwork and get a new body, right?"

"But who would want him out of the university for a week or so? The only thing that's changed is Ms Pickett teaching the night class. Why would that be so important?" Harriet was stumped.

"The university is practically empty at night, anything could happen. Maybe she needed an excuse to be there," Connor said dramatically, the effect was somewhat spoiled by the subsequent sip of his drink, with which he came away with whipped cream on his nose.

His words rattled in Harriet's head, though.

Harriet would have loved to have said the email came through at that moment, because it would have much better served the dramatic tension. However, the email came through almost half an hour later, when Dan had gone back to work, and Harriet and Connor had moved on to the topic of their dissertations, although the email was no less chilling after the conversation they'd had earlier.

Dear Students,

Due to unforeseen circumstances, Mr Jones will not be returning to his teaching post for the foreseeable future. This means all of my lessons henceforth will be held in the evening. If there are schedule conflicts with this, please let me know. Also, all previous students of Mr Jones will have to come and see me for a chat about their coursework thus far.

–Ms Pickett

Chapter Four

Harriet wasn't convinced that Ms Pickett shot Mr Jones, for one, the shooter was decidedly male. Despite the fact she hadn't seen his face, he was somewhere on the brink of six foot, and barrel chested. About as far from Ms Pickett's rail-thin form as could be. Connor had been insistent that if you were going to shoot someone, you'd hire a shooter who least matched your own physical description.

Harriet had hummed, but secretly disagreed. Ms Picket definitely gave off the vibe of a strict headmistress; it was all too easy to imagine her in a high collared dress with frills, but for the same reason, Harriet didn't think she would be the type to hire an assassin so she could sneak around the university at night without suspicion. The woman seemed too proper for anything shady.

The next class they had with her was tense and was only a few days later. Harriet and Connor sat at the back of the class, in the far-right corner. They had shifted their desks slightly closer to each other, so it would be easier to pass notes between them. Connor insisted she was a witch, not a werewolf, and wouldn't be able to hear them, but Harriet insisted that Connor could be heard by a deaf person, let alone Ms Pickett, who may not be a werewolf but could probably hear a pin drop across a music concert.

All throughout the lesson they eyed Ms Pickett and speculated why she might want to get Mr Jones out of the way so she could have an excuse to hang around in the evenings. Connor's suggestions got more and more ridiculous as the lesson went on, until they almost got caught because Harriet choked on her laughter when Connor suggested she was having a midnight love affair with a student. Harriet could not imagine the prim woman to let anyone near her with that kind of intent; she looked like she'd rather claw your eyes out.

After Ms Pickett continued on with her lesson, with her eyes darting suspiciously to them on occasion still, they continued trading notes. Harriet felt like she was back in school, when she had finally persuaded Cora to come to university with her; they were Harry and Colin, trading notes at the back of the class.

"I need to go talk to her about my essay plan, now that Mr Jones isn't coming back in time," Harriet told Connor, once the lesson had finished. The noise of them speaking was covered by the noise of frantic students trying to leave the lesson.

"Okay, I'll wait outside. You said you were going to the coffee shop after, right?"

Harriet nodded, "I brought my essay plan to work on, if you don't mind."

Connor said it would be fine, and that he could do with working on his.

They agreed to meet on the benches outside the English block, and Harriet went to the front to see Ms Pickett.

Harriet could see why Connor thought she was a witch. She didn't have the pale pallor of a vampire, nor the hair and bulk of a werewolf, and she had wrinkles around her eyes and mouth; demons didn't often include imperfections when creating their bodies. And to have a human teaching at a supernatural university was even more unusual than having a human student. Although Harriet was now leaning to believe that there was something not-human about Connor.

It would also explain her smiling at the girl she was currently talking to, who was clearly also a witch. Although smiling was probably a bit far, her scowl looked less severe than normal, and her being a witch would also explain her distaste of Connor in particular, who she pulled any excuse to reprimand. Witches had the worst relations with humans, mostly because they had the most clashes through history. They also held favouritism strong; witches ran through family lines and therefore had networks spread throughout their ranks. Everyone knew everyone, even more so because around here they lived in small Welsh towns.

She didn't think Ms Pickett was necessarily a bad person for it, although it did make Harriet even less inclined to trust her, even more so than your basic distrust of witches. Connor said he was sure it was in the realm of possibilities that she was up to no good. He said he'd been dealing with her for the last two years of his degree, and her favouritism ran deeper than just friendlier smiles but extended to grades as well. Ms Pickett's favourites had a tendency to do well on essays and exams; due to her giving hints or marking leniently, no one knew for certain.

"Miss Aukland," Ms Pickett said. "What can I do for you?" The way she said it made it sound like 'What do you want?'.

"In your email you sent out, you said we needed to run through our essay plans with you now that Mr Jones isn't going to be marking them."

Ms Pickett nodded and held out her hand for the paper, which Harriet deposited it in, taking care not to directly touch Ms Pickett's hand, for fear of having her eyes scratched out.

"Yes, this looks fine. Just remember to link each point back to the essay question." She had barely scanned her eyes over it before handing it back with the most generic advice possible. Harriet resisted rolling her eyes and wished Mr Jones hadn't been shot in the head.

"Right. Thanks." Harriet grabbed her bag and made her exit. At least Connor was coming to the coffee shop; she could bounce ideas off him. He might have some idea about what style of writing Ms Pickett favoured in her essays.

When she reached the exit from the English building, she couldn't see Connor on the bench as planned. She went and stood by it, hoping to see if he'd wandered off a bit.

She went to send him a message, asking if he was already at the coffee shop, she hadn't been long, but the moon was fairly high in the sky already and the temperature had dropped several degrees since entering. Being probably human, he would definitely feel the cold.

On her phone was a message from him, it read:

Saw someone dodgy. Meet me behind psych building when you get out.

She couldn't believe he'd wandered off in the middle of the night to chase a dodgy looking, most likely supernatural being. She cursed under her breath and took off in the direction of the psychology building. She made sure to keep to the outskirts of the path through the uni, and detour around the back of the building but Connor wasn't there. She edged along the side of the building, where she found Connor, crouched amongst the bushes along the front of the psych building.

She went to reprimand him, but he clamped his hand over her mouth, his wide eyes told her to keep her mouth shut when he removed his hand. He held up both his hands either side of his head in a clawed fashion and gave a silent mock growl, before pointing at the man waiting by the Social Sciences building that was opposite.

Harriet doubted the man was a werewolf. If he were, he would have been able to hear them approach, given how quiet the campus was at this time. He could just look a bit like a werewolf; he was tall, quite hairy, and barrel-chested.

Harriet froze.

This could totally be the shooter. She went to tell Connor before remembering she should stay quiet, just in case. She grabbed her phone and typed out her suspicions, before turning the screen to show Connor.

Connor typed back on his phone, *He's the shooter?!*

He could be, I didn't get a look at his face.

Connor's interest doubled and he started shuffling closer to get a better look at the man. Harriet noticed he was wearing smart clothing and could pass as another lecturer if he had been wearing a lanyard, but he wasn't, which meant he must have snuck passed reception. Reception being one vampire who guarded the entrance at night. He was also carrying a briefcase. No one who carried a briefcase in the middle of the night was innocent, but that was mostly based on murder mystery shows.

Suddenly, Connor started hitting her arm to get her attention; his other hand had slapped over his own mouth to stop any noise escaping.

Harriet followed Connor's line of sight to see Ms Pickett striding over toward the man.

She stopped a few steps away and they had a brief and terse conversation, before Ms Pickett handed over a USB stick. The man took it, slid it into his pocket and retrieved a piece of paper from his briefcase, which he handed over to Ms Pickett. Ms Pickett shoved it into her laptop bag. The two shared an awkward glance, before turning and going their separate ways, the man at a casual stroll, and Ms Pickett scurrying from sight.

Once they were both out of earshot, even allowing for werewolf super hearing, Connor let out a massive gasp.

"That was so unbelievably dodgy!"

Harriet couldn't disagree with him; there was everything suspicious about that.

"Ms Pickett just met up with the shooter and exchanged information!"

"I don't know if it was the shooter. Lots of men are six foot and broad, but I don't know, there was something about him that just made me immediately think of the shooter."

"That's got to be damning, right? She has to have organised his shooting!"

Harriet was hesitant still. Ms Pickett just didn't seem the type to shoot someone to get the out of the way, she seemed far more likely to get somebody sacked through academic, above board standards. Although Harriet couldn't deny that it looked ridiculously dodgy.

"She definitely has something to do with all this. It can't be a coincidence," Harriet mused. "Come on, let's go to the coffee shop." Connor had started shaking with the cold, and the coast was most likely clear.

*

Connor talked Dan's ear off with what they'd found out about Ms Pickett, whereas Harriet kept quiet. It was lucky that the coffee shop was empty, apart from them.

"You were so right. She wanted Mr Jones out of the way, so she could meet with this burly dude," Connor told Dan.

There was something niggling at Harriet. The way Ms Pickett had headed straight for the man. The practiced ease in which they'd made their exchange gave her the impression they'd met up before. And if they'd already been meeting at night at the uni, there was no need to get Mr Jones out of the way.

Unless Mr Jones had accidentally stumbled upon their meeting, and seen something he shouldn't have. He would have to walk by the psychology building to get to the staff car park from the English block.

A chill went through Harriet; maybe Ms Pickett was capable of something like that after all.

She hurried to the table to tell Connor her theory, almost forgetting to take her order with her.

She explained what she thought, about them having met before and the possibility of Mr Jones come across the scene, and therefore needing to get him out of the way.

"Ms Pickett may not even have known, if the burly dude took matters into his own hands."

"True," Connor nodded, having already scoffed his brownie, and eyeing her food. She slid the muffin towards him, and he continued speaking, muffin crumbs flying out of his mouth. "And of course, they'd be no footage of it all."

"What do you mean?"

"The courtyard between the psych building and the social science building is notorious for not having CCTV. Some student disabled it last year and no one has fixed it yet. All the students know. People are forever doing exchanges of test answers and stuff, drinking alcohol and such."

"Do any teachers know?" Harriet couldn't believe she hadn't heard of this before.

"I imagine so, it's not a well-kept secret, but if the teachers pretend they don't know, they don't have to fix it, and also they know exactly where to find all the students swapping papers. If they announced they knew, people would find some other secret place to do it."

"So, it's possible Ms Pickett knew about this spot?"

Connor nodded. "Highly likely," he said, around a mouthful of muffin.

"I think it's time we had a word with Mr Jones." Harriet was determined to get to the bottom of this now. Having a teacher cavorting with a possible murderer did not sit well with her.

"How are we going to find him?"

"I have a friend at the library," Harriet grinned, feeling more settled than she had in days.

Chapter Five

Simon was a nerdy looking guy. He was thin like Connor, but also on the shorter side and wore thick glasses. Harriet had met him in the mid-1800s, before women were allowed to attend universities. Harriet and Cora had been masquerading as men, and Simon had cottoned on. He didn't sell them out, but he was interested in why they'd wanted to attend.

Eventually they'd all met; after all, three vampires at the same university, they were all using the same shadowy hiding spots and were bound to meet eventually. Harriet had explained to him that after 220 years, she was getting bored with needlework and cooking. She wanted to know what the male half of the population were up to and she'd quickly powered through most of the books in the local library, which was more of a shelf.

Cora had not been very old at that point, having only been about 20 years since Harriet had bitten her, and she'd only been mid-twenties then. They found out Simon was not too old himself, a mere 90 years old, but he said there was rumours of another vampire not too far away, who was said to be around 700 years old. Vampires were far and few between; it was startling that three of them were in the same place. Harriet hadn't realised there were more than a handful of them until the reveal, when hundreds came out.

Ironically, the vampire who was 700 years old that Simon had once spoken about with such admiration, ended up the dean of the university Harriet attended and the university library Simon now worked at. The tone he most used to describe her now was muttered and included lots of swear words.

"Can't believe it!" Simon grumbled. Harriet could hear him practically from across the room, although it did make him easier to locate.

"What's wrong?" Harriet asked when they got close enough.

"Oh, Harriet it's you. The dean hired a new librarian and he's completely inept. I'm having to completely reshelve all of these," He gestured to the laden down cart in front of him.

"Ouch, well I won't take up too much of your time, I just need your help with a small matter." Simon eyed her suspiciously but didn't interrupt, "This is Connor, he's in my class, I'm assuming you heard Mr Jones got shot?"

Simon nodded, "This isn't going to get me in trouble is it?"

"No, I mean probably not, we're just wondering if you could help us find Mr Jones."

"I'm assuming he'll be at his house, sorting out his new body," Simon said, his eyes narrowed as he looked between Harriet and Connor, "Why do you want to know, anyway?"

"We think we know who his shooter is," Connor said, before Harriet elbowed him in his stomach.

Simon sighed, as if he knew that was coming. "Shouldn't you be going to the police with that information?"

"We don't know for certain, and we have a theory, but we'll need Mr Jones to confirm it."

Simon rolled his eyes. "I mean technically yes, I have his address on the system, but I could lose my job if I gave it to you. Besides," he eyes darted around to make sure no one was about, "I think he may have been mixed up in something."

"That's what we think!" Connor said excitedly, but Harriet looked at Simon's shifty expression.

"No, we think he witnessed something. What do you think he was up to?"

Simon let out a sigh and slumped against the cart next to him. "I mean, I don't know, and I don't want to speak ill of the, well, he's not dead, but speak ill of the murdered, but he'd been checking out weird books for a while."

"What books?" Harriet and Connor asked.

"Normally, he takes out books on the English language, or journal articles," Simon's voice got even quieter, "but for the last couple of weeks, he's been taking out law books, history books about supernaturals, and a couple of days before he was shot, he was looking up policies about supernatural beings, everything that got put in place after the reveal. I think he got into some kind of trouble and was seeing how the law protects him."

"Can we borrow these books?"

Simon shook his head. "He took them out, and obviously hasn't been able to return them, since, well, he was shot. Most of them we only have one copy of. The history book I think we have a couple of copies of. I can get you that one.

Although you were there for what most of the book covers." He directed the last part to Harriet.

"I'd like to borrow it," Connor said. "There's not a lot of reliable information about it online. I didn't realise you had information here that wouldn't be online." Harriet realised Connor was still rattled over his discovery of the labs after the reveal.

Simon smiled. "Yes, most of the things on the Internet are sensationalised for clickbait, but this history book in particular was a written account by Sabina, the dean of the university. She's almost 900 years old now. It's very thorough, and a bit gory on the details. She didn't spare a thought for the weaker stomachs of her readers." Simon and Harriet shared a smile, "She had a few copies made, but all of them belong to the university."

"Thanks, I'd like that." Simon smiled again and went off to find one of the copies of the book.

"We need to get Mr Jones' address. I'm going to run to the computer and grab it off the system. You distract Simon if he's back before I am," Harriet said, edging towards the front desk.

"It's probably password protected. How are you going to get in?"

Harriet scoffed. "Simon has had the same password since his first computer. I'll be back in a minute." And with that, she darted behind the corner, back to the front.

Connor shifted awkwardly, and several slow minutes passed as he waited for either vampire to return. He was getting ready to go find Harriet, when she pulled up next to him, slightly winded.

"Got it. He seriously needs to change his password." She waved her phone in his face, and he breathed a sigh of relief as Simon rounded the corner from the opposite direction, brandishing a battered, heavy looking book.

"Worked in our favour, didn't it?" Connor muttered before Simon got too close to hear, "Thanks, man. I've got some serious reading to do."

Simon grinned. "Come on. I'll sign it out for you and let you on your way. Just be careful with it. If this gets damaged, Sabina will be out for my blood. If I had any, at least."

When they reached the desk, Simon scanned everything through. Connor handed over his university ID and then received it back. It was when he was about to remove the book off the circulation desk that Simon placed a hand on top of the book, stopping it and Connor. Simon's eyes, however, were fixed on Harriet.

"Any particular reason, by the way, that I was already logged in to the system when I got here?" His tone was light, and so was his hand on the book, so Harriet figured he couldn't be too mad.

"Not sure, maybe you forgot to log out?" Harriet didn't even bother to try and sound innocent; it hadn't fooled Simon in a long time.

"Don't let her be a bad influence on you," he said to Connor, "God knows she dragged me and Cora on enough wild goose chases."

"Excuse me," Harriet said, "He dragged me into this one."

Simon sighed, "And yet you're about to stalk down your English teacher."

Harriet huffed, "He piqued me interest, I'm curious now."

"Nothing more dangerous than a curious, headstrong woman." Simon smirked.

Harriet rolled her eyes; it was something a lecturer had said to them, back when they'd first met. Cora had been careless with her disguise and been caught as a woman on university grounds. Harriet had caught up with them and said Cora was her girlfriend and had just wanted to see the university. The lecturer had warned 'Harry' against headstrong women who snuck into universities, and they both had broken down in tears when they recounted it to Simon. He'd always subsequently referred to the two of them as his 'curious, headstrong women'.

"Just don't do anything stupid, okay? And when you inevitably do it, don't tell me about it, and then I can't be accountable."

Harriet rolled her eyes, "Yes, yes, fine. Connor and I will have the fun, and you stay home. And don't forget to log out this time." She laughed at Simon's indignant expression.

"I'm sorry, by the way," Connor said, when they hailed the bus outside the campus.

"For what?"

"If you feel like I dragged you into this thing with Mr Jones." Connor looked a bit shifty at the topic when they sat down on the bus, but there weren't many people on it at this time.

"You didn't drag me into anything, it's just fun to rile up Simon a bit. He was always the most reserved out of the three of us," Harriet said, not wanting Connor to feel bad. He had dragged her into it a bit, but to be honest, she probably

34

would have found a way into trouble anyway. "I used to drag him and Cora out on wild goose chases all the time, sneaking into places or sticking my nose where it wasn't wanted. I haven't done it in a while, they are both off working now, and I thought it wouldn't be the same doing it without them."

"Why don't you do it with them anymore? Dan says you always come to the coffee shop alone, but Simon works at the university."

Harriet wondered when Connor and Dan had spoken without her there, "I— yeah, I mean, I see Simon, but he works nights, and we can't go out during the day, so we mostly just speak when I go to the library."

"And Cora?"

"Cora didn't like university as much as me and Simon. She went for a couple of degrees, but she decided she wanted to work instead and started at a factory during the First World War. She's been working ever since. It's been hard for her to climb the corporate ladder when you can only work night shifts, so she's been trying to set up her own company recently, so I haven't seen her much."

Connor nodded, looked at the book in his lap, "I didn't even think about the wars."

Harriet made a questioning sound.

"I mean, I was listening to what you were saying about Cora, but I didn't even think that you must have been alive during the World Wars. I kind of forget because of you looking young."

Harriet laughed. "It happens, I got into an argument with a history teacher once about the Boer War, before the reveal. I couldn't tell him how I knew he was wrong."

"Did you fight?" Harriet thought he meant with the teacher at first, before realising he was still talking about the war.

Harriet shook her head. "No, no women allowed, not that I could have, anyway. Registering becomes particularly difficult if you don't have a birth certificate or any ID that isn't forged. Unis don't look that close at them; the army does."

"Damn, you must have had to change names and towns often then?" Harriet nodded. "And the dean! She's, what, 900? How many times do you think she's moved?"

Harriet grinned. "Have you met the dean?"

Connor shook his head, and Harriet smirked. It was the smirk of someone who was laughing at your expense, and it was funnier to keep you in the dark.

"What do you—"

"So, what are we going to say to Mr Jones then?" Harriet hurried on, still smirking. "Before we were going to ask him if he saw Ms Pickett, but now, Simon reckons he might be in deep on his own."

"Why don't we ask him about Ms Pickett, then see if he changes his story when we imply that we know about his dealings? Pretend we know more than we do. See what he says."

"Perfect."

The bus dropped them off on the other side of town. "Right, we need to be quick about this," Harriet said, looking at the time on her phone. "Sunrise is in four hours, and the bus will take 40 minutes to get back near my flat."

"Okay, let's find out what's been going on," Connor nodded and set his shoulders in determination as they headed to the street Mr Jones lived on. He was still clutching his library book to his chest, and Harriet could see his knuckles were white where he was holding it so tightly. Connor had been reading it for the latter half of the bus ride, and his eyes had slowly been getting wider and wider in horrified fascination.

They knocked on the door and rang the bell several times to no avail.

"He might be asleep?" Connor suggested, pressing and holding the bell again for several seconds, for good measure.

"He's a demon. He doesn't sleep." One final press of the bell.

"We might have to come back tomorrow," Harriet sighed, kicking at the step.

"Or, I mean," Connor hedged, "I think I heard a noise."

Harriet frowned. She hadn't heard anything, "It sounded like Mr Jones might have fallen over and we should really make sure he's okay."

Harriet grinned. "How are we going to get in, though?"

Connor pointed to the slightly ajar window. Mr Jones lived in a tiny detached up and down, and the window led directly into his living room. "Mr Jones should really properly lock his windows at night."

Harriet grinned in return at Connor; they were definitely a bad influence on each other. At least Simon and Cora had somewhat tempered her.

Perhaps her friendship with Connor wouldn't be the same as her one with Simon and Cora, but still nice nonetheless. She grinned to herself as she clambered through the window and into Mr Jones' living room, it was certainly interesting.

Chapter Six

The room was dark when they entered, which meant Harriet ended up sprawled across the floor, along with the several stacks of books she'd knocked over when she'd entered.

Connor followed, and managed to avoid her, but knocked over several more stacks of books, which apparently lined the windowsill, saving on the purchase of a bookcase and a burglar alarm. If Mr Jones hadn't heard them before, he certainly had now.

The two straightened up, and prepared for the footsteps coming from the bedroom, but nothing came. Harriet hesitantly turned on a lamp that sat in the corner, casting a low, warm light across the whole room. The room looked no different than most student accommodation, sparsely furnished and slightly battered looking.

Harriet and Connor quickly started piling books back to their places on the windowsill.

"Hey," Connor said, "this is the history book he got from the library," holding up a book identical to the one in his other hand.

"Great," Harriet said, glad that it hadn't been damaged or covered in muddy footprints by their entrance.

"I wonder if the rest of the books are here," Connor started riffling through the pile of books on the floor.

Connor was making enough noise to wake the neighbours. Harriet wanted to tell him to be quiet, but she was distracted by the fact that Mr Jones was clearly not here to hear them. She looked around and saw there was a fine layer of dust on most of the surfaces, she stood up and started looking for the kitchen.

There was obviously no need for any food for a demon, as they didn't possess any of the needed organs for digestion. Often, though, they would keep basics, in case someone visited. Coffee and tea usually, but occasionally the more popular demon might stock long-lasting milk, tins of food and biscuits.

Mr Jones was not one of those demons. All that was in his kitchen was more textbooks and journal articles, some beer mats, but no beer or any other kind of drink and a poster about the upcoming Christmas festival in town, most likely having been shoved through the letterbox, given its creased appearance.

However, her voyage to find any mouldy food led her back through the hallway, where there was a stack of letters piled up on the floor. Which confirmed her theory that Mr Jones had not been home in a while. She snuck upstairs to check his bedroom and the whole room was covered in dust. Although most demons' bedrooms are laid out more like an office, as they have no need to sleep, unless the room came with a bed, they often lacked one. Although Mr Jones' bed did look reasonably rumpled and still had papers scattered across it, as if he found marking more comfortable on the bed, opposed to the desk.

Harriet took a closer look at the papers and found they were the essay plans they'd handed in a week before Mr Jones was shot. Indicating Mr Jones was a most likely a procrastinator, and most definitely hadn't been home after he'd been shot, or at least, had left shortly after.

She went back downstairs, less careful of being quiet now. She stopped by the front door and grabbed his mail. She found Connor still in the living room. He had replaced most of the books but was left with a small pile in front of him still.

"Where did you go?" Connor asked, eyes wide and darting, as if he thought Mr Jones was about to pop out from behind the sofa, demanding to know why they'd broken into his house.

"Mr Jones isn't here. I reckon he hasn't been here in a while. These were stacked up by the door." She started sifting through them. "What are those?" she asked, gesturing to the pile of books in front of Connor.

"These are all the books I can find that are from the library. Simon was right, a lot of these are legal rights books, like, a lot of them." He picked up well over half of the books to illustrate his point. As he picked them up, something fell loose from one of the books, and Harriet had a brief moment where she thought they'd torn something when they knocked them over and Simon was going to kill her for damaging a book. Connor noticed too. He quickly put down the stack of books and grabbed the damaged one. Although it wasn't actually damaged when Connor opened it, he found what had come loose was in fact a letter. It had already been opened but the letter had been stuffed back inside. As far as Harriet could tell, Mr Jones had been using it as a bookmark.

"I don't recognise the company," Connor said, handing over the letter to Harriet, who dumped all the other letters on the floor.

The logo was a picture of a building, maybe a university, which had a blue ring around it saying, 'scientia ipsa potentia est'.

"How's your Latin?" Harriet asked.

"Non-existent. How come you don't know it?"

"Because I've lived in England for the last 500 years, not Rome in the last millennia. I know some Latin words, but no more than anyone couldn't guess. Like scientia, it's going to be science, knowledge, or learning."

"So, you reckon the building is a school?"

"Possibly." Harriet flipped the envelope over and took out the letter.

"You know it's illegal to open someone else's post," Connor said, although it sounded more like he was reciting a fact rather than giving her a warning.

"Also illegal to break into someone's house; besides, the letter was already open." The letter was on heavy, thick paper; expensive. The letter looked quite formal and was nothing more than a thank you for his contribution to their cause. Harriet threw it back on the ground and sighed. Nothing.

Connor picked it up and scanned through it, "You reckon he donated something, lab equipment or such, but he was an English teacher."

"Maybe he assisted them with research or something," Harriet said, going back to the letters she had previously discarded.

"Seems a bit weird he'd hide it in a book, though."

"What makes you think he hid it? Could have been a bookmark."

Connor shook his head. "No, there's already a bookmark in this book, and the letter came from the very back. It's just a couple of blank pages there."

"Huh," Harriet said, having found another letter from the same place. "When is that letter dated?"

"About a week before he was shot. Why?"

"Because I've found another letter from the same place, but this one was unopened by the door." Harriet opened the letter and found it had been dated only a few days ago.

She scanned the page:

Unfortunately, Mr Jones, we cannot on this occasion rescind the data you have provided us. It has already been processed and can no longer be altered.

Apologies,
Mrs Colton.
Magic Supervisor
Collian Ltd

"What research do you reckon he was doing? Must have been dodgy if he wanted it back," Connor said, after reading it himself.

"But why send it off in the first place? He must have discovered something and changed his mind. What data can you not 'rescind'? Surely you can alter data after the fact?"

"Would have thought so," Connor agreed. "Just some numbers on a screen, you could definitely discount some. Who do you reckon this Mrs Colton is? Reckon she's a witch?"

"Probably, with a title like that. What I don't get is why Mr Jones was working with witches; didn't trust them as far as he could throw them."

"Why?" Connor asked, with the trepidation of someone knowing their species is probably going to come out of the story looking like an asshole.

"Demons are made of magic, right?" Connor nodded, "Except they're not, they're made of something we don't understand, that science can't explain yet, so it's given the umbrella term of magic, and that's that, but then witches started spreading this old folk tale about a woman who used her magic for so much evil that a council of witches took her magic off her and the unattached evil magic became the first demon. Which all demons disagree with, because they aren't actually made of the same stuff as witches, but because science can't explain either, they get lumped in together. It's another reason no one likes humans very much. And why demons and witches don't get along."

"Is that why you don't like witches?"

"I—" She always tried to treat witches the same as other supernaturals, but she didn't trust them, "Why do you think I don't like them?"

"You always make this sour face when they get mentioned." He squinted his eyes slightly and pursed his lips, "Like you're trying not to frown."

"I don't trust them because they don't trust anyone. Witches run in family lines, all this hereditary magic closeted away for generations, and all the knowledge with it. Covens only know the magic that has been in their family lines. Two covens could use magic completely differently because they don't share with each other."

"So you don't like them because they fight with each other?"

"No, I just don't trust anyone who covets knowledge just so they can be the smartest person in the room. Plus, witches are hoity toity intellectuals who think they're better than anyone else. Knowledge shouldn't be constrained by the few, to disadvantage the masses." It was what an old professor had told her; she'd always suspected he'd known more than he let on, although he could have just known about her being a woman.

"Makes sense, I suppose. None of the witches in my class will even speak to me."

"Because witches and covens are all about family lines, it's often run on old-school networks, which mean favouritism, favour and exclusivity are all the rage with that lot."

Connor nodded. "I've definitely experienced that." His eyes drifted to the clock on the wall as the two of them drifted into silence; not an awkward silence but definitely not comfortable. Connor swore loudly.

"What?"

"The time, we've been here ages. It's almost sunup." Connor hurried to his feet, balancing the pile of books in his arms.

This time Harriet swore loudly. She stuffed the letter in her coat pocket, and they both scrambled out of Mr Jones' flat, leaving the not-quite-awkward silence behind them as they hurried for the bus stop.

*

Harriet managed to reach her flat with three quarters of an hour to spare, although that was still cutting it slightly too fine for her.

She was about to head down to her flat, specially built underground flats for vampires too paranoid for blackout curtains, when her hand found the letter she'd stuffed in her pocket. She fiddled with the edge of it, before quickly heading instead to the ground floor, more specifically to the flat that resided directly above hers.

41

Theirs was a flat of four, three witches in the same coven, and one long suffering werewolf, who Harriet passed on her way to the flat and granted her access without having to buzz in. Linda, the werewolf, was used to fielding angry complaints about the coven, and their endless explosions of trial potions. It was unusual to experiment outside the realms of what was taught in your own coven. Although nothing about the three male witches was common, mostly notably that they were all male, and not related to each other. Most magic ran down female lines, although it was not completely unheard of to have male witches, it was more unusual. More remarkable was that they were friends, and not family. Harriet had heard rumours that they'd separately been banished from their covens, either for being male (usually only the traditionalist covens abided by this), or for experimenting with spells, and sharing information with outsiders. Harriet wasn't sure what was definitively truth, but all of them certainly had an affinity for creating spells.

The werewolf was in running gear, which still did little to explain her departure from the flat; Harriet didn't know anyone who went running at four in the morning. A loud bang like a gunshot went off. Harriet startled but Linda rolled her eyes and gave an apologetic look before heading off. Harriet felt sorry for her poor super hearing living with these three, although she supposed it saved buying an alarm clock.

Harriet followed the noise to the communal kitchen, and her empathy for Linda increased tenfold when she saw the state the kitchen was in. A giant cauldron sat in the middle of the room, and vials and beakers were littered across the countertops, either cracked or containing mysterious liquids. There was also a stack of small Tupperware containers, each one filled to the brim with herbs.

A jovial face peered out from behind the Tupperware, his dark hair standing on all ends. "Heads up!" he called, "What's the problem? Sorry about the noise, Linda's taking the noise complaint letters to reception tomorrow, if you've got one." He pointed to a pile of at least six or seven letters, which were pinned down with a beaker that was dripping its contents onto the paper.

"Um, no. I had a question for you, actually," Harriet said, drawing her attention towards the now bubbling over cauldron, in the hopes that the witch would follow her eyeline. He stood his ground, still smiling broadly. Harriet watched the contents drip onto the carpet and sizzle; she really hoped that it wouldn't make its way through to her ceiling.

"What can I do for you?"

"I'm Harriet. I live below you guys. Just wondering if you could look at a logo for me. I think it might be a company run by witches?"

"Liam." The man smiled, and held out his hand to shake, but it was covered in ingredients of some kind, so Harriet purposefully misunderstood and dropped the letter on it instead.

Liam didn't seem deterred. "Gosh." He blew up his cheeks with air before slowly releasing it. "I've never seen it before. Hang on. Hayden! Jack!" He shouted in the direction of the hallway.

Two identical shouts of "What!" called back.

"Come here!"

Two lots of doors slammed open and then closed, and two sets of footsteps approached the kitchen, along with joint grumbling.

"Yeah?" A redhead and a blond peaked their heads around the door.

"Hayden, does this logo look familiar?" Liam handed the letter over to the redhead, Hayden. The other witch, who must have been Jack, wandered over towards the cauldron, the contents now slipping quickly down the sides. Jack didn't appear concerned, however. He just grabbed one of the Tupperware boxes and threw half of it in. The liquid quickly simmered down, and Jack nodded to himself and set the Tupperware down on the nearest surface, without bothering to fix the lid back on.

"No, sorry," Hayden said before handing the letter to Jack, "Liam said you reckon it's a company run by witches,"

Harriet nodded. "Possibly a research facility or someplace dealing with data."

When all three witches were stood in front of her, she could plainly tell none of them were related; they all had different skin colours and hair colours, but all of them had that wild-eyed look of children up to no good, and all their hair was messy and stood on end, like they'd been sticking forks into toasters before she arrived.

"Sorry, I don't recognise it. Alice might…" Jack said, and the other two joined in insisting that if anyone knew it was Alice. Harriet asked who Alice was after it became apparent that none of them were going to elaborate.

"Oh, she runs a supply shop in town. Hang on, I'll find the address for you." He scrawled it on the back of one of the noise complaint letters and handed it over to her. "Alice is part of the Walters coven. Big family, and she keeps her ear to the ground. Alice knows everything." All three witches nodded.

"Um, thanks," Harriet said, sceptical about going to a large coven about this. It was already risky showing these three a letter that clearly did not belong to her, but she figured if they were creating their own spells and potions, and were outcast from their own covens, they had to been skating fairly close to illegal activity anyway.

She pocketed the letter and the address, with no intent of following up on the latter.

"Thanks," she grinned "I'll let you get back to your—" She waved at the potion.

"Thanks," they replied, and as she left, she heard the snippets of the lads' conversation.

"I'm going back to bed. Wake me up when that turns purple. And not lilac like the last goddamn time!"

"Lilac is totally purple!" she heard Liam defend before the door to the flat closed firmly behind her.

Well, it was certainly an interesting visit, if unproductive. Harriet yawned, and climbed into bed as the sun started rising.

Chapter Seven

Several days passed and all the happened was Sabina, the dean of the university, had emailed Harriet, requesting a meeting with her during the week.

Harriet was paranoid that it was going to be about breaking into Mr Jones' flat, despite the fact there was no way Sabina could have possibly known about that. It was most probably about how her dissertation was coming along, in light of the fact that her lecturer and dissertation supervisor had been shot and banned from stepping foot on university grounds. Sabina had subsequently taken on all of Mr Jones' dissertation students.

Harriet liked Sabina, she was cool and collected, making sure to gather all facts and sides of the story before casting her opinion, and she still managed to install fear into people despite how she looked.

Most people, hearing there was a 900-year-old vampire, instantly imagine a wrinkled beyond belief and frail form. It had surprised Harriet when she'd first met the woman and seen a stern looking child in the office chair.

Sabina apparently had become a vampire aged eight, after being infected by an older girl who hung around near her house. Harriet had read the book Sabina had written. Apparently, she had never seen or heard from the girl again, and is now the oldest living vampire known today. Harriet wondered what became of the older girl, why she decided to pick Sabina and then leave.

"How are your studies coming along, Harriet?"

"Very well." No matter the number of times Harriet conversed with Sabina, it always made her slightly uncomfortable, looking across the desk and seeing a child looking at her over her steepled fingers and with a serious expression. It gave her pause when she realised this is probably why people got so uncomfortable when she referenced experiencing something well past her look of 20 years ago.

"Remind me what your research is on, again?" Although Harriet had no doubt Sabina had checked everything over before she had arrived.

"How language has developed, relating to humans' language about supernaturals before and after the reveal, specifically in and around North Wales."

Sabina hummed. "Are you enjoying it?" Harriet nodded. Sabina seemed to sense she wasn't making any headway into easing Harriet into whatever she wanted to say.

"I have recommended to all of Mr Jones' students to book an appointment in with the support councillor. Watching someone get shot can be a very traumatising matter," she said.

Harriet nodded in agreement, but knew she was not going to be attending support sessions. She'd seen far worse in her time; witches aflame, and during her brief few decades in France, public guillotining was a popular choice.

Sabina knew this, and going by the knowing look in her eye, she wasn't going to push the matter. She and Sabina went through her progress on her dissertation project, and where she was hoping to be in the next few weeks. Throughout the entire meeting, Harriet could feel the letter burning a hole in her jacket pocket.

When she was dismissed, she almost upended her bag in her haste to get to the library.

"Ugh," Harriet said to Simon, as soon as she got to the main desk. "What is it about Sabina that makes me believe the myth that vampires can read minds?"

"Tell me about it," Simon rolled his eyes, "She always knows when I've been slacking off, and reading, anyway, Cora and Connor are through there. I'm on my break for the next 15 minutes so I'm joining you."

Harriet raised one of her eyebrows as they started walking over to one of the tables at the back, for a bit more privacy.

"My interest was piqued." Simon said flatly, but he had that twinkle in his eye that reminded Harriet of the good old days. They really needed a voice of reason in their group. She'd messaged Cora a few days ago, after she'd decided resolutely that she wasn't going to be visiting this Alice witch. She still needed more leads on this research facility, and Cora was the next closest thing, working in business. She could only hope a facility run by witches was supernaturally unique enough to be well known in business circles.

"That can't be true," Harriet heard Connor say as she and Simon neared the desk. Harriet suspected that Cora was winding him up; it was a game they used to play after the reveal, see who can get a human to believe the most ridiculous

46

vampire fact. Harriet stopped when she realised misinformation was going to bite them in the ass.

"Uh huh," Cora teased. She had a young face and could easily have passed as a teenager: rounded cheeks that used to be rosy before she turned, and wild curly hair that was now tightly held in a bun. She was wearing business casual clothes and would have looked professional; if it weren't for the relaxed slouch she was sat in and the wide grin on her face, you could easily place her having a drink with her friends at the bar.

"Cora!"

"Harriet!"

Cora got off her seat and came round and hugged Harriet, "You haven't changed a bit," she winked.

"Your sense of humour hasn't either." Harriet sat down next to Connor. Cora resumed her seat across from them, and Simon joined her. She hadn't seen Cora in person for more than a passing conversation in at least five years.

"So, Connor said your teacher was shot, and so you broke into his house," Cora said, grinning. "You definitely haven't changed."

Harriet rolled her eyes. "There's more to it than that. Ms Pickett was being incredibly suspicious. The new English teacher," Harriet clarified at Cora's confused look. "And Simon here said Mr Jones was taking law books out of the library, like he was in some sort of trouble."

"Right, so what do you want me for?"

"You messaged a while back saying you got a job at a start-up company."

"Yeah, PA to an entitled bore," Cora said. "But if it gets me noticed by the higher ups, then thank god, it's supernatural friendly, in case you were wanting to make this degree your last," Cora trailed off. She'd been trying to persuade Harriet to leave education since she did.

"I may as well make it up to a nice round forty degrees," Harriet teased, and Cora made a face back at her. "Anyway, I was wondering if you could have a look at this logo and tell me if you recognised it?"

Cora nodded and took the letter. Her eyebrows jumped. "I do know it."

"What is it? We think it's run by witches," Connor added.

"It's a small research facility. I don't know if it's run by witches, but a high portion of their staff are magic. I don't know what kind of research they do, but I can look into it."

"Please," Harriet said, taking the letter back, and putting it back in her coat pocket.

"Will do," Cora looked at her watch. "My break was only for half an hour. I better be off."

"Will anyone actually be at the office at this time?" Simon pointed out, given the fact that it was one in the morning.

Cora nodded. "As I said, it's supernatural friendly. We have a whole group of vampires who carry on the work at night, including my floor supervisor," she laughed, and waved as she went back to work.

"What do you reckon?" Connor asked.

"Hm?" Harriet was watching Cora leave, hoping it wouldn't be another five years until she saw her friend.

"Do you reckon we have enough to confront Mr Jones? Go back to his flat?"

"Considering we went to his flat with the same intention before, and we had half the information we have now—"

"Which still isn't a lot," Simon interjected.

"We probably should," Harriet finished, glaring at Simon.

Simon merely added, "Didn't you say the flat hadn't been occupied in ages. How do you know he'll be back now?"

"I-um, may have visited the police station yesterday," Connor hedged. "Well, I'd been reading that law book about supernaturals that I borrowed from Mr Jones—"

"And that will need returning to the library," Simon said, and then yelped when Harriet kicked him under the table. "When he's finished reading it, obviously."

"Of course, I'll return it. Anyway, I wondered if Mr Jones was being held illegally. You said that one officer was being really rude to him," Connor said to Harriet, "So I went down and acted really annoying, kept going on about Mr Jones needing to look at my research paper, just on and on, eventually the guy said he wasn't here, and that I needed to leave." Connor looked inordinately pleased that he'd been kicked out of a police station.

"Great, we'll go now then," Harriet jumped up, and Connor followed.

"Don't do anything illegal." Harriet raised her eyebrow at Simon. He huffed. "More illegal than you've already done."

"No promises," she called out behind her and she and Connor took off towards the bus station.

They made their way through the window much more quietly this time. They had knocked initially, but there had been no response this time either. As soon as they climbed through the window, Harriet could tell someone had been in the house recently, other than Connor and herself. There were fewer books on the shelves, and most of everything had been stripped bare. Two large suitcases sat in the middle of the living room. On top of them were documents, a new passport and driver's license, and a plane ticket.

"Connor, he's leaving," Harriet whispered.

Connor came over and looked at all the documents. "His plane ticket was bought the day after he was shot. I don't think he was ever planning on coming back to the university."

"Do you reckon he was using his new face to escape whatever dodgy shit he's landed himself in?"

"Maybe I suppose whoever shot him in the face did him a favour then," Connor joked.

Harriet hummed in agreement.

"What are you two doing here?" Mr Jones called out from behind them.

Harriet and Connor spun around to face the man; documents still incriminatingly held in their hands. Mr Jones no longer looked like Mr Jones, although his face matched the one on the passports, so Harriet figured it was safe to assume it was him. He was much taller now, well over six foot, had long floppy brown hair, and had a gun held loosely in his hand.

"Mr Jones! Sorry, we were just, just wondering—" Now Harriet was stood in front of him, she didn't know whether or not she could accuse him to his face, even if it wasn't the face she was used to.

Connor stepped in, "What research were you doing for that facility? And why do you want it back?"

Mr Jones' wide eyes fixed on Connor, "What do you know about that facility?"

Harriet could tell that Connor was trying to come up with an off the shoulder response that made it seem like he knew more than he did, but he ended up flailing for words before eventually settling on, "We know you sent them data, and then asked for it back."

"Do you know what the data was?"

Connor shook his head. "Was it the same data on the USB that Ms Pickett had?"

Mr Jones looked confused, "Ms Pickett? From the university?" Harriet and Connor confirmed, "Why would she—"

A loud bang interrupted Mr Jones' train of thought. Harriet nearly jumped a mile; it sounded like someone was trying to break the door down.

Mr Jones swore and hurried his words. "If you know what's good for you, you'll stay out of it, the whole business. Seriously, stop looking into it."

Supernaturals were no different to humans, in the sense that, if you told them not to do something, it was a sure fire way to get them to do it.

"Now hide!" Mr Jones hissed at them, Harriet and Connor stared at him in horror as he faced the door and raised his gun.

He must have noticed the lack of movement from behind him, as he turned and shooed them again, "For God's sake, *hide*!"

Harriet and Connor both scrambled to find a place to hide, particularly as most of Mr Jones' stuff was gone and left the room rather empty. They found a broom cupboard under the stairs and hid in it; they could hear the wooden door splintering as whoever it was continued hammering the door. Eventually, they heard one massive, and final sounding crack, a moment of silence, and then heavy footfalls of boots.

"Jones. Put the gun down. We wouldn't want anything unfortunate to happen. Now, would we?" The man who was speaking had a deep voice, and it was severely unpleasant. He sounded like the kind of man you wanted to punch in the face because he was so smug.

Harriet tried to crack the door open to see who it was, to find out if he looked like Mr Jones' shooter, Connor frantically waving in the cramped space to stop her. She could see about six men, mostly their backs, as they were all facing Mr Jones in the living room, all of them stood with the stance of military men. Harriet wondered what the hell Mr Jones had gotten himself into.

"No, we wouldn't. Look I'll keep my mouth shut, I swear. You won't hear a peep out of me. Just let me leave and I'll start over, somewhere new. I promise," Mr Jones begged.

"Sorry. Boss' orders."

Harriet couldn't quite see what happened in the resulting scuffle, but she heard Mr Jones yelp, and a clatter that could only be his gun hitting the floor, before the men made their way back into the hallway where her view was better.

Just in time for her to see what must have been Mr Jones with a bag over his head, being dragged off into the night.

"Grab his stuff and meet us in the car."

Two of the men cleared up the suitcases and all of the documents and took the last trace of Mr Jones out of the flat.

As soon as the door slammed closed, Harriet and Connor raced to the window to watch as Mr Jones was kidnapped off into the night.

Chapter Eight

"What the hell was that?" Harriet said. The black SUV, and wasn't that the ultimate suspicious, bad guy car, had rounded the corner and disappeared into its surroundings.

"I think Mr Jones just got demon-napped," Connor was stood with his mouth ajar; Harriet was tempted to reached over and shut it, but the comic gesture didn't feel right in light of recent events.

"Okay, what do we do? Do we follow?" Connor shook his head. Harriet supposed they'd already had a decent head start and it was unlikely they were going to catch up on foot, not to mention the danger of trailing kidnappers.

"Well, we definitely know he was up to something dodgy," Connor said.

"And also, that Mr Jones clearly had no idea about Ms Pickett," Connor sent a confused look her way. "He was definitely surprised when we said her name. I don't think he was lying."

"So, if Mr Jones didn't see something he shouldn't have, then what is Ms Pickett doing?" Connor said.

"Maybe it was innocent, after all. Maybe she was just having a secret lovers' meetup."

"With the exchanging of USB sticks? Very romantic."

Harriet rolled her eyes. "I don't know if I can deal with two English teachers being separately dodgy. Maybe it's a requirement, must have English degree and interest in illegal activity," Harriet snapped sarcastically.

This time Connor rolled his eyes. "Maybe it's to do with Mr Jones' unknown dodgy research? Maybe Pickett found out, got her hands on the research, and gave it off in USB form."

"What on earth could be so enticing about English research you'd kill for it?" Connor shrugged a response, "I reckon we try and get our hands on that USB stick."

"From Pickett? Are you mad? I'd rather face those army blokes with the guns."

Harriet noted Connor also thought they were from the army, as she hadn't voiced her suspicion to him yet.

"Fancy a coffee? I definitely need some sugar." Connor looked so tired. Harriet didn't have the heart to remind him it was sunup in a few hours.

"Sure."

They stepped through the wreckage of the door. No need to bother with the window when there was a perfectly good gap of splintered wood right there. They started walking down the street, heading to the coffee shop. They failed to notice another black SUV idling discreetly halfway down the road.

*

"You broke into the man's house?" Dan said in disbelief. Harriet had only stepped away for a moment to call Simon and update him on what had happened, but in that time, Connor had managed to get through most of the story. Harriet rolled her eyes and wondered how he hadn't stumbled over his words; he must have been talking so fast to get them out.

Harriet liked Dan but she didn't know if they could trust him fully with what happened. Simon and Cora were bound by friendship not to send her to jail. Although Harriet knew that Connor came here without her sometimes and was better friends with Dan than she was. Hopefully Dan wouldn't go to the police if it meant Connor would go to jail. He must have been there a lot because Dan didn't glare at him as much as everyone else, either that or he'd opened up to Connor quicker than Harriet had ever seen.

It had its perks. Dan now gave them free brownies whenever they were in, which was most days after their lectures. Or rather, he gave Connor brownies, but Connor was nice enough to share.

"I still don't think you should have broken in. What if someone saw you? They'll think you're both tied up in this now."

"No one saw us, don't worry," Connor grinned as he took his hot chocolate, but lingered by the counter while Dan made Harriet's coffee. "So what's the plan now?" he asked when Harriet reached the counter.

"I reckon we still need to work out what the facility is, and what Ms Pickett is up to."

"You can take Pickett," Connor scoffed.

Harriet gave him a flat look, and continued, "I asked the coven who live above me about the facility, and they didn't recognise it, which is why I called Cora, but they did say there was a woman named Alice who might know something. As much as I don't like the idea, they said she keeps her ear to the ground. If there's a facility that hires a load of witches, she might have heard of it."

"Okay. I thought you didn't trust witches?" Connor said.

Dan handed over her coffee, and said quietly, "Alice isn't too bad, for a witch."

"You know her?" Harriet and Connor both asked.

Dan nodded. "She's got a shop down the street. She's part of an old coven but she's got a more modern approach to magic. There's a group of them, Gen Z witches." He rolled his eyes subtly at the name. "But they believe in expanding knowledge through exchanging information and experimenting with testing the limits of new spells and such. I think they just like blowing things up."

"How are they still in covens if they're pushing for change?" Harriet asked.

"I don't believe their covens know they're doing it."

"So how do you know?" Connor said, beating Harriet to the question.

"My little sister is friends with one of the witches. They both spend half their lives at the shop. I usually get roped in to picking them up when they've bought too much and their bags are too heavy," Dan started, picking at the frayed edge of his apron. It was a forest green colour and had 'Full Moon Coffee Shop' stitched onto it. Harriet wondered who had picked the name, because she doubted it was Dan.

"I reckon we visit her tomorrow. What are her opening hours?" Harriet asked, having a suspicion about what the answer might be.

"9 am to 5 pm," Dan said, and Harriet winced.

"I can go on my own if you want," Connor said, suddenly realising what the problem was. "I could record everything on my phone, so you don't miss it."

"No, it's—it's okay." Although it wasn't really, Harriet was so very tempted to take him up on his offer, just wait back at her flat, in the safety of the windowless concrete walls. However, she didn't like the idea of Connor going and asking a witch invading questions without backup, not that she thought the witch would do anything to harm him, but witches, like most supernatural creatures, did not like humans.

"I could go with him," Dan volunteered quietly. "She'll recognise me at least, it might put her at ease a bit more."

"We could definitely do with you there to help reassure her we're just nosy, not dangerous, but I should come too. I'm too involved in this now to abandon ship because of a little sunlight."

"So how are you going to do it?" Connor asked.

*

Harriet was glad that at least it was winter, and therefore multiple layers would not look completely out of place. Also, that she lived in a town where the majority of the population were supernaturals and so it wouldn't look too weird. She still felt like an absolute tool when she caught sight of herself in the mirror, though.

She had thick, and slightly loose-fitting jeans, with high socks and large boots. She had a long sleeve top, covered by another long sleeve button up (done all the way to the top), gloves, a scarf that was wrapped round up to her nose and a beanie pulled as low down as possible without obstructing her eyesight. She also had a coat that went down to mid-thigh and an umbrella at the ready.

She dithered by the door for a full 10 minutes, the stub of what used to be her little toe seemed to prickle with nerves, although Harriet was positive she was imagining it.

She received a text from Connor, saying he and Dan were outside. Dan had offered to drive them, even though it was a short walk. He said it would save her being out in the sun for extended periods of time. She had heartily agreed.

She took several steadying breaths and left her flat. She had the umbrella held low over her head, so it blocked out the sun on her face and subsequently almost walked into the car door that Connor had opened for her. She could feel the heat of the sun warming the fabric of her jeans and it made her want to turn tail and run back into the safety of her building.

Connor helped her into the backseat, somehow managing to close the umbrella enough to get it in. Dan had fixed small blankets to the windows in the backseat, and the rear window to minimise the light that was coming in, but she still wanted the umbrella to block it from the windscreen.

"Okay, you okay?" Connor asked, when he got back into the passenger seat and they headed into town.

"Yeah," Harriet said, in a breathless and high-pitched voice that was the opposite of how she'd intended it to come out.

"We can still turn back if you want," Dan slowed the car at Connor's words, as if he were prepared to do that the second Harriet agreed.

"I'll be fine," Harriet said, although it was mostly for her own benefit. The car sped up again. "Two hundred years inside. I could probably do with some fresh air," she mostly muttered to herself.

"So how did you get around unis before the reveal?" Dan asked from the front seat.

"Most of the classrooms were set in the same building as the accommodation. Then all you need to do is cover as much of yourself as possible and stick to shadowy corners. Sometimes when it was harder, I'd forge doctor's notes about a skin condition, then more recently online classes and night classes got introduced and it was easier. Then supernatural unis made it easier again, there was always a way around it. Cora never liked it, though, said it was too much effort. Me and Simon didn't mind, though."

The car came to a gentle stop, and Harriet realised Dan had gotten her to talk to stop her from over thinking and panicking about the sun. She was both annoyed at being treated like a child scared of needles, and also weirdly comforted.

"Okay, that wasn't so hard," she said to herself. Now she just had to get out of the car again; that was going to be the tricky part. She got her umbrella at the ready as Connor came and opened up her door.

Chapter Nine

When they entered the shop, after much manoeuvring to get the umbrella through the door, it was empty.

"Hello?" Connor called out. Harriet found the darkest corner of the room, which was stood in the shadow of a large cabinet and folded her umbrella up. Witches were a superstitious bunch.

The shop was small, or rather, it was spacious but stuffed full of things, making it feel cramped. The low ceilings and high shelves didn't help its case.

Harriet had never been in a witches' shop before, and so wasn't sure exactly what they were supposed to sell. Surely, they couldn't make much money considering how secretive they were.

"What do they even sell?" Harriet asked aloud.

"Herbs, ingredients for potions," Dan said, his nose was wrinkling. Harriet thought the smell of incense was strong for her; she couldn't imagine what it would be like for a werewolf.

"And books with the basics, that every magic user should know." A girl appeared from behind the counter, she clearly worked here. "It's on the back wall over there, if you're interested." She directed towards Connor, who immediately headed for the back of the shop.

"We also sell the tourist trap stuff for humans, do palm reading and future telling," Harriet got the impression from her tone that she didn't like that aspect.

"Could we speak to Alice?" Harriet asked, Dan opened his mouth to say something, but the girl beat him to it.

"I am Alice. Hi, Dan."

"Hello, Alice." Dan said.

"Oh." The girl looked no older than sixteen she had wild ginger hair, and her face was mostly comprised of freckles.

"We were wondering if we could ask you a few questions."

Alice's stance shifted, "About what?"

"We were wondering if you recognise this logo." Harriet moved forward to hand over the letter.

Alice coughed. Harriet would almost swear she had a smirk on her face. "No, sorry. What is it? I might know it by name."

"We think it's a research facility that is employing a lot of witches. We're trying to find out more about it."

Alice paused. "Hang on, I'll be back in a minute."

As Alice ducked into the back, a sleepy black Labrador wandered through into the shop, followed by a younger, more awake one.

"Oh my god, they're adorable!" Connor said, having appeared from the back of the shop, only now clutching a book that looked as if it was falling apart. Connor ducked down so he was eye height with the dogs and started enthusiastically petting them.

Dan looked hesitant. Most dogs were confused by the canine sense they got off werewolves, but some got aggressive, so werewolves had learned to be cautious when approaching.

The younger lab, however, bounded straight up to Dan and Harriet and started sniffing them, before allowing a cursory pat from each of them, and then headed back behind the counter. The older lab, who was grey around his muzzle and slightly overweight with age, was content to sprawl on the floor and receive attention from Connor. It was unusual for a witch to have dogs, the preferred familiar being a cat, but Harriet supposed if you were a dog lover it could work just as well.

"Is this the employee list of the witches who work there?" Alice asked, back behind the counter with a piece of paper in her hand.

Harriet took the paper; despite the fact she had no idea about any employee list. It was a list of nine names, none of them had the same surname, so lower chance of them being related.

"Who are these people?"

"They're missing persons, more specifically, missing witches," Alice said.

Harriet didn't recognise any of the names, but she also wasn't up to date with the local covens.

"My sister knows her," Dan said. "Lucy, she's gone missing?"

Alice nodded sadly. "She's our friend. She went missing a week ago. It's when I started looking into it and asking around that I found out about the others."

"You think it has something to do with the research facility? We only suspect witches work there because apparently Mrs Colton is the Magic Supervisor there, whatever that means."

"I've not heard of her, but I can ask my mum. She might have. It was only because you said it was employing a lot of witches, and no company I know of employ witches en masse. Most witches avoid corporate companies. It was just a hunch," she said. "Covens round here are getting angsty, panicking about retribution," she chuffed, as if the idea were ridiculous, but she was still worried about it.

"Retribution from what?" Dan asked.

"Others covens. Around here, most witches my age have started questioning holding on to secrets, wanted to set up more inter-coven relationships, and the older coven members don't like it. Most of our parents questioned it, and so they don't mind us taking a bit more action, but it's their parents that are the problem, want us to 'honour the old ways'," she mimicked. "Bunch of superstitious hags, didn't even want me to have a dog as a familiar. Edna pitched a fit when Lucy got a tabby cat as a familiar."

"You think the older generation are kidnapping witches?" Dan asked.

"I don't know, all I know is Lucy had a fallout with her coven about her familiar, and her hanging out with me, and er—" She bit her lip, "And her hanging out with your sister, because she's a were." Dan frowned. "And when I was asking around, Holly's sister said she'd fallen out with her gran the afternoon she disappeared. Some dispute about not using Archaic Latin."

"You think that was enough for her gran to kidnap her?" Harriet asked. "Is Latin really that big of a deal?" Then again, Harriet didn't think a tabby cat was that big of a deal.

"Yeah, even I don't use Modern Latin, although I'd never care about someone else using it."

"And you think they're being kidnapped by their grans, and what? Sent off to work at the facility?"

Alice shrugged, "I thought I'd check, just in case, but if you're already looking into this demon person, maybe you could look into this too?" She said hopefully.

"Two mysteries to solve!" Connor said excitedly. "We should open a detective business."

"I'll help," Dan said, "Not with the detective business," he added when Connor let out a whoop. "I can try and find Lucy and the others, and I can see if Madison knows anything about before she disappeared."

"Thank you, you'll want to check out the club as well." Dan lifted an eyebrow at Alice's statement. "Quite a few of the girls were there before they disappeared. It's a nightclub on the dodgy end of town, it's for demons and witches." Nothing like suppressing years of tension and fighting with bad club music. Harriet supposed that was why the Eurovision song contest was still going.

"How am I meant to check it out then?"

"You'll need an invite from a witch or demon, but you can get in," Alice said.

"Why didn't the police look into it? If a load of the girls went missing after being there?" Harriet asked at the same time Dan said, "You haven't taken my sister there, have you?" His eyes narrowed dangerously at Alice.

Alice scoffed derisively, "I'm not stupid enough to take an underage were to a dodgy nightclub, and the police did no more than a cursory glance over the place. They're morons."

Connor and Dan both seemed on board with helping Alice track down her fellow witches, although while Dan seemed in it to help his sister, Connor seemed more in it to help his burgeoning detective business, but Harriet had a more pressing matter. "Okay, but what about Mr Jones? Are we not going to work out what happened to him first?"

Connor hedged. "Well, it did look quite dodgy, and if he's really dodgy enough to get himself shot, do we want to help him? I mean, we can still look into it, but don't you think we should help the missing girls first? They haven't done anything wrong."

Harriet didn't like it, but it did make sense. Mr Jones was incredibly suspect at this point, but it just didn't seem to add up with the jovial lecturer she'd had for the last two years. She was aware enough that she was in this mostly to try and redeem Mr Jones in her eyes, but a string of missing innocent girls was probably more worthwhile than a possibly corrupt teacher.

"Okay, have you got the information about the girls written down anywhere so we can have a look through? You said you spoke to their families?"

Alice nodded. "I've got recordings, I'll send them to you." She got her phone out and waved her fingers around in front of it until her magic opened the phone and found the files. Harriet questioned the necessity of doing that. Why couldn't she just use the phone regularly? *Witches*, she mentally rolled her eyes.

After Harriet, Connor, and Dan had exchanged numbers with Alice and been sent the recordings, Connor grinned excitedly and said, "So when are we all going clubbing? And more importantly, what is everyone wearing?"

Chapter Ten

Harriet had obviously been clubbing before. She'd been a student for around 200 years now. She was definitely familiar with clubbing; she just hadn't done it in a while. And while she was sticking glitter to her face in half-moons on her temples, she felt very much like a mum trying to be 'cool' and hang out with her child and their friends. Grumbling about kids these days, glitter and short skirts.

Harriet was less concerned about her skin showing at night, but there was always that worry that she wouldn't get back in time, so she kept tugging on her skirt, trying to make it longer.

She'd left her hair down and was wearing a long sleeve red top, but her legs were completely bare between her boots and her skirt. She was debating investing in some thigh high boots and tights when she got a text from Connor saying that he and Dan were outside.

They had decided to get to the club as early as possible to maximise their time there. It was currently nine o'clock, and the club had only just opened for the evening so there shouldn't be too much of a crowd at that time.

When she hopped in the car, sans umbrella this time, she noticed both the guys dressed nicely, Connor in a tight long sleeve blue shirt, and Dan in a black button up.

"Damn, we scrub up nice," Connor echoed her thoughts.

The drive didn't take long, and it was filled with Connor's excited chattering. Harriet wondered if he'd been on a night out during university, seeing as he hadn't made friends on his course due to them all being witches, and she'd never heard him mention the people he lived with.

Harriet had slightly more patience for his rambling after that.

Alice met them at the front of the club, and they made idled chatter while Dan drove off to find a parking spot. She was dressed to the nines, in a 50s style dress with her red hair up in a complicated quiff that must have required at least two dozen bobby pins. She also had perfected her makeup and looked far older than sixteen. Harriet had wondered how she had been getting into the club, although she supposed there was also a fake ID involved somewhere. She also seemed to have brought her familiar with her and had even clipped a bow tie to his collar. Harriet supposed a club for witches was probably more lenient on familiars coming, although it was an odd sight.

When Dan got back, they headed to the front door. There was barely a line this early, so they quickly reached the front. The sign for the club hung overhead, 'Magic'. Dan snorted when he saw it. "Original," he said.

"Says the man who owns 'Full Moon Coffee Shop'," Alice shot back, although Harriet thought she may secretly agree with him, given the small smile on her face.

"Madison named it when she was ten," He grumbled, "She thought she was being ironic."

Alice smiled at her friend's antics and didn't say anything back. By this point, they were level with the bouncer.

"Full name and coven, if applicable," The guy on the door said in a bored voice, not even looking at the ID Alice presented.

"Alice Walters, Walters coven," Alice recited. Harriet peered at the small electronic pad the bouncer was holding; it just seemed to have a list of names on but no ages. Harriet supposed it was plausibly deniability and the club didn't care enough as long as they got trade.

The guy glanced over Harriet's pale skin, Dan's bulk and hair, and landed on Connor, "Full name and coven, if applicable."

"Ur," Connor stuttered, glancing at Alice, who just continued smiling as if nothing were odd. "Connor Manning, urm, not part of a coven."

The guy clicked around on the screen. "Not registered," Connor gave Alice a betrayed look before the guy cast some spell at Connor, nodded and gruffly said, "If you're new in town, you need to register with the Magic registry office in the town hall. In you go." He nodded at them all.

Alice marched in confidently, and the rest of them followed, more than slightly confused as to what had happened.

"So, what does everyone want to drink?" Alice asked when they got to the bar, oblivious to the confused stares the other three were giving her. "What? Why is everyone so quiet?"

"Why did he ask me for my name?" Connor asked. "And then tell me I need to register?"

"Why haven't you registered? I thought you went to uni here? Anyway, it's one guest per magic user, and these two are obviously a vamp and were."

"Stereotypically so," Connor rolled his eyes.

Alice laughed, "I meant aura wise."

"But I'm not a magic user," Connor said, not letting the issue go.

Alice pulled up short, "What? But I thought—"

Connor shook his head, "No, I got told I had a spark by a druid when I was 10, but no one else would hear the time of day when I tried to pursue it."

"You've definitely got magic, though. It's in your aura. And that spell the bouncer did was a detection spell, fairly basic, anyone could do it," Alice insisted. "I know I'm a bit more in tune with auras than your average witch, but even so. I suppose they might have thought you were taking the piss, especially with you being male."

"So, you're saying all this time all anyone had to do was a simple spell, but no one bothered because they thought I was mocking them?" Connor asked in disbelief.

"Dan noticed it as well," Harriet pointed out.

"Yeah, but the only reason was because he said he was human, and I thought he was magic," Dan said, "and I only brought it up with him because you were both talking about it, and I didn't think he'd be offended if I mentioned it. I wouldn't have said anything otherwise. Especially to a new customer."

"Yeah, you just hadn't built up that witty rapport you have with your regulars," Harriet teased. Dan glared at her.

"I—people either thought I was joking, or they were too polite to say anything, that's what you're saying," Connor said, partly horrified. "I need a drink." He flagged the bartender down.

"So, what does my aura tell you?" Connor asked Alice, after they'd all put their drink orders in.

"There's a small amount of magic, until I heard you speak, I thought you were a little kid, that's why I suggested the beginner's book of spells."

Harriet was confused. Surely Alice would have been able to tell Connor wasn't a child by looking at him, until Harriet started paying closer attention and realised Alice's eyes, while they looked alert, and would look at you while you were speaking, they didn't move around or glance at anything, as if she only turned to look at you to make you more comfortable. Harriet realised her familiar was also her service dog. Alice was blind and Harriet was an idiot. No one could know how long it took her to realise. Moments were starting to come back to Harriet. Alice asking her to tell her about the facility, rather than looking at the logo and using her magic to open the right app on her phone. Harriet was fairly sure if she had enough blood in her system for it, she would be scarlet with embarrassment.

"But I don't look like a little kid," Connor said, "Oh my god, you're blind." He seemed to be going through the same process as Harriet, although his thought process seemed to also be coming out verbally.

Thankfully, Alice laughed. "Don't worry about it, a lot of people don't realise at first." She was addressing both Harriet and Connor, Harriet didn't know if she had guilt in her 'aura', whatever that was. Dan just looked like he couldn't believe it had taken the pair of them so long. Their detective business wasn't taking off anytime soon. "It took Dan throwing a book at me, and it hitting me in the face for him to realise."

Dan looked horrified. "It was the first time I met you! I thought you'd catch it," he said defensively.

Harriet and Connor started laughing, although they waited until Alice laughed, to make sure they weren't going to offend her.

Their drinks arrived, they'd all ordered a cocktail except Dan, who'd ordered a whiskey. Although Harriet's was the only cocktail that was a Bloody Mary with actual blood. Connor grimaced slightly when he saw it. "Who puts celery in a drink?"

Harriet, Alice, and Dan all snorted, and the conversation moved on, although Harriet did remember to ask Alice later about auras. It was two or three cocktails later, so the answer was slightly more jumbled than she wanted.

"Auras are like magical auras, so I can tell if someone is a witch, or not, but vampires and werewolves are different from humans. I suppose it's like a sense of smell for werewolves. I find I'm better at reading auras because I use it more," Alice said enthusiastically, "Each person is slightly different, but mostly fall into their species category. For example, I know Dan's signature specifically because he picks Madison up from the shop. He and Madison both have the aura of a wolf, but they both have a slight variance, and therefore I have learned to tell them apart."

"And Connor?" Harriet asked. She'd never heard witches talk about aura as anything more than a gut feeling, '*I don't like the feel of his aura*' and such.

"He just has the aura of a young witch, who hasn't quite come into their magic yet; hasn't practiced and grown their magic. Magic is like muscles, the more you work it, the stronger it is."

"So, you think he's a witch because your aura thing told you?"

"He's not quite a witch, similar to a young witch but not. Like, even if you never practiced magic, it would still be stronger than his is now as it will also grow with you, and then grow expone—expenent—it will grow on top of that if you practice."

"So, he's not a witch," Harriet said, and Alice just shrugged.

"He's something," she settled on, which seemed to be the default answer everyone who came across Connor said.

*

Another cocktail later, and Connor asked Alice why she couldn't fix her eyesight with magic. Harriet and Dan both swung their heads round to him and gave him wide eyed looks that hopefully conveyed, 'You can't ask that!'.

"If it was medical, I might be able to find a witch who is a doctor to fix it. Otherwise, it's like trying to perform surgery on yourself, and I'm not a doctor. But it's not even that. It's a neurological disorder, there's nothing wrong physically, and no witch worth her herbs would go poking around in the human brain with magic, don't know enough about it." Once again, Alice hadn't seemed offended by Connor's questions, although she did seem quite drunk.

"Huh," Connor said. He was slumped in his seat, and Harriet's theory about him not having gone on a proper night out was starting to hold water, considering how much of a lightweight he was.

"But enough questions about me, what about you?" Alice cooed the last word. Harriet couldn't believe how drunk she had gotten. Although Harriet had giggled in response, she looked in betrayal at the almost empty glass in front of her.

Alice just kicked her feet out and rested her head heavily on her hands, elbows propped on the table. Her dog, named Petal, had been snuck up onto the booth they were sitting in, the floor being far too sticky.

Connor and Alice seemed to be exchanging life stories they were in such deep conversation. Dan was the most sober out of all of them, him being their

66

lift home. Werewolves had a faster metabolism so could drink more, but they could still get drunk if they had too much. Dan had stopped after three anyway.

Harriet grabbed her glass and wiggled it at Dan before heading up to the bar. "Back in a minute," she said.

*

Harriet wasn't sure how she had got chatting with the man at the bar, but she could see Dan in her peripheral, glancing at them occasionally.

The man was late twenties maybe, quite good looking, although not Harriet's type. Tall and with brown hair and a sad expression. She could almost hear Cora's voice in her head, talking about picking up strays.

"I don't know. He was meant to be here, and I haven't seen him in days," the guy complained into his drink. He was a demon, but he must have created a body with a functioning digestive track, otherwise he'd need to spit that drink back out. Most demons didn't bother, but those who did were usually found around bars or restaurants, enjoying themselves and their working organs.

"Who?" Harriet asked, having lost track of the conversation in a drunken haze.

"Neil. My friend. He was meant to have a drink with me. We always come here on a Friday."

"Where do you think he is?" Harriet asked, waving to the bartender for two more drinks.

The man, Harriet's drunken brain thought he might be called Geoff, shrugged, "Haven't seen him since last Friday. We had a drink and he left with some chick," the guy moped.

Harriet patted him on the shoulder, "Womaniser?"

The guy let out a surprised laugh. "No, definitely not. Shyest guy in the world. Anyway, he was upset because he'd fallen out with Sammie." He said it as if Harriet already knew who Sammie was, maybe he'd mentioned her before. Harriet couldn't remember.

Something niggled at the back of Harriet's head. She couldn't quite grasp a hold of it because it was sloshing around with the rest of the alcohol. "Was he a witch?" she asked. She wasn't sure why, but it felt like the right question to ask.

"No," Geoff said. "Demon."

"Oh," Harriet said, disappointed for some reason. "I'm sorry about your friend."

They both toasted to Neil. "I hope he messages you soon!" Harriet cheered.

*

"Connor! Connor, come back here!" Dan called, as Connor laughed, dodged his grasp and took off, running down the street. Dan took a second to look between Connor halfway down the road and heading for a crossing, Harriet and Alice stumbling slightly behind him.

"Stay here," he said, before running off to wrangle Connor back.

Harriet and Alice laughed. They leaned on each other as they headed in the same direction at a slower pace. "I'm sorry tonight was a bust," Harriet said.

"It's okay. Probably shouldn't have drunk as much," Alice said. She had Petal on one side and Harriet on the other, so she didn't veer too far off course.

"I didn't see anyone dodgy, but we could have checked the CCTV!" Harriet pouted.

Alice shrugged. "Police would have checked it when they investigated, they may be incompetent, but I think they would have had to do something if they saw a kidnapping."

"True, we should go back, though, and properly have a look around."

"Okay," Alice agreed decisively.

They watched as Connor came running back towards them, Dan having cut the distance between by well over half. Harriet wondered how Connor had managed to outrun a werewolf in jeans that tight.

Dan caught Connor just before he reached Harriet and Alice. Connor was by far the most drunk and had a madly infectious grin on his face. Dan tucked him under one arm angrily, while muttering about wrangling toddlers.

They walked Alice to her house, and she waved goodbye to them cheerily. Harriet vaguely wondered what time the shop was going to be open tomorrow.

They had walked Alice home as she had lived surprisingly close to the bar and Dan hadn't got anything in his car to safely transport her dog with. So, after they had dropped her off, they headed back to the car. Dan watched through the rear-view mirror as Harriet and Connor fastened their seatbelts. Once he was satisfied, he started driving. Harriet drifted off before they arrived.

Chapter Eleven

Harriet had been clubbing a lot, but hadn't been drunk very often. As a vampire you needed to drink blood to be able to digest the drink and absorb the alcohol into the bloodstream, and before blood packets became readily available, it was simply too difficult to get enough blood to survive on, let alone drink recreationally so you could get drunk. Harriet had never wanted to steal from blood banks or hospitals so she had never had the opportunity until around 20 years ago, and by that point Cora had stopped attending uni and even Simon had started work, albeit at the university, but neither could afford to go out drinking that much because of night work.

All of this led to the simple fact that Harriet had forgotten how bad hangovers could be. Her head was pounding, her mouth was beyond dry and she had to squint her eyes in the harsh light. She jolted when her brain finally caught up, frantically trying to shuffle into a shadowy corner somewhere. It was only when she noticed the lack of pain and smell of burning skin that her brain calmed enough for her to take in her surroundings.

She was in a large, low ceiling room with no windows. There was also a lot of boxes, some labelled 'Christmas stuff', others 'Halloween box' and so on. She realised she must be in someone's basement. Possibly Dan's. She vaguely remembered Dan herding her and Connor through a front door.

She was currently sat on a mattress, still in her clothes from last night. She sat up feeling woozy still when Dan popped his head around the door.

"Morning," he smirked, putting a mug of blood in front of her and a plate with bacon sandwiches on it. "Sorry about the basement. We didn't have any blackout curtains in the guest rooms."

Harriet nodded, before putting the cup on the floor next to her. "I think I've had quite enough blood for now." She did feel bad, though. He probably had to go to the shop this morning to get that.

"You threw up most of it when you came back in last night. Scarred Madison. She thought you were human and dying."

Harriet laughed quietly. She could well imagine it. She must have been rosy cheeked from blood and looking incredibly human like. She had probably taken in the majority of the blood, though, as she could still feel her heart pounding in her chest.

She took a bite of the sandwich. "I'll have some later," she promised, before Dan started fretting at her, although he seemed more the type to angrily glare her into taking care of herself.

Dan nodded, "I'll send Connor down. He's been awake a couple hours."

Harriet nodded absentmindedly. Dan actually gave a small smile, although Harriet didn't know why.

She found out several minutes later when she heard Connor's approach before he'd reached the top of the stairs. He was apparently the type of person that wanted everyone to know how bad his hangover was, forgetting everyone else also had a hangover.

"Why do I feel so terrible?" he said, slumping on the mattress next to her.

She pulled the duvet higher over her and snuggled down a bit more, and just moaned in agreement.

"So," she said, "What did we learn last night?"

"That you shouldn't drink tequila."

Harriet huffed, but thought rolling her eyes might cause her to throw up. "About the case."

Connor groaned, "Do we have to do this now?"

"Yes, because instead of properly looking around last night, we just got drunk, and I can't leave here until later." Harriet paused, "Actually what time is it?"

"About four in the afternoon." Connor rolled over, and faceplanted his head into the pillow.

"Okay, so I vaguely remember this guy at the bar, Greg, Geoff, Gavin, somebody, and his friend went missing, hadn't seen him in days."

"Mm?" Connor reply came from the pillow.

"But—" Harriet said, struggling to remember what it was he'd said. She had been quite a few Bloody Marys deep at that point. "I don't think his friend was a witch, though. I think he said he was a demon."

Connor rolled slightly so Harriet could see half of his face, including one raised eyebrow. "A demon, who would kidnap demons?"

"I don't know if he was kidnapped, but it does seem a bit of a coincidence, doesn't it? Loads of witches go missing from a bar, and a demon hasn't seen his friend in a week at the same bar."

"True, maybe. I suppose it is a witch and demon bar. Text Alice, see if any demons have gone missing."

Harriet doubted whether any witches would care about demons going missing, but Alice seemed to have a more modern outlook on these things, and if it helped locate her friends, she supposed Alice might be more inclined.

Are demons going missing as well as witches?

Harriet sent the message off, Alice had given Harriet her number last night, and told her that her phone read out her messages so she could text as well as call. Harriet noted that Dan must have charged her phone upstairs and put it back at some point before she'd woken up, because it was now fully charged, which it certainly hadn't been last night.

Not sure, hadn't checked, will have a look – A.

Alice replied promptly. Harriet wondered if she'd opened the shop this morning, and what her parents had said. Although if Alice's regular trips to the club hadn't pinged on their radar before, Harriet doubted that they would care now.

"She's not sure. I wonder if any vampires and werewolves have gone missing," Harriet said, the thought coming to her quite suddenly and it filled her with dread. She hadn't thought to consider whether or not different species had been going missing. "Connor." She turned, and Connor was halfway back to falling asleep. Harriet, however, was frightfully alert now, "Connor! I need you to go and ask Dan if he's heard of any werewolves missing recently, whether or not they'd been at the club."

The club might not be their only kidnapping hotspot. Who 'they' were, Harriet didn't know.

"Why?" Connor moaned.

Harriet pushed as hard as she could to turn him over until he was squinting in the light and glaring at her. "I will pour this mug down your throat if you don't wake up properly now. What if they're opening the labs back up?"

Connor sat up, "I thought those labs were totally illegal."

"They are now, but I doubt they'd ask permission. It just seems too much of a coincidence that witches and demons, and maybe vampires and weres are being kidnapped. No matter what Alice says, I don't think that anyone is kidnapping their granddaughters because of a bit of Modern Latin, unless there's some evil knitting circle out there somewhere."

"Oh my god." Connor stood up quickly. He looked vaguely green, whether from the sudden movement or from the thought of the genetics labs dissecting teenage girls. "I'll go talk to Dan." He made a rocky journey up the stairs.

Harriet sat there, fiddling with the duvet uneasily. Before giving up and grabbing her phone, she dialled Simon's number.

She had to call three times before he picked up the phone, "Who the— Harriet? It's four in the afternoon. What are you doing up?"

"Simon, I need your help, I need you to find out if any vampires have gone missing recently."

"Why? More importantly, how? As I previously stated, it's four in the afternoon. Despite popular expectation, I don't live at the library. I'm stuck in my flat until you are." Simon was always grumpy when he was woken up. Normally so was Harriet, but the drinking had messed with her sleep schedule somewhat.

"But like, do you know anyone who might know that you could call?" Harriet wasn't even in the mood to bite back.

Simon seemed to pick up on this, and hesitantly said, "Anyone who would know is also going to be a vampire, who might not be at their most cooperative at this time."

Harriet sighed. "Okay, but can you call as soon as you've had a talk around?"

"Will you be telling me why you want to know?" Simon asked, with the undertone of 'You will tell me'.

"I mean I don't know for certain, but quite a few witches have gone missing, and maybe some demons, and so I just wanted to check about vamps and weres, because if they're all going missing, it would suggest, well, it would suggest that someone might be trying to open the labs."

There was a pause on the other end of the phone. "That's quite a leap. I'm not saying it's not true, but people and supernaturals go missing all the time. It's just statistics."

"But a lot of them have been going missing from one particular club, Magic. It's on the other side of town from the uni."

"I've heard of it, and you don't think that maybe drunken supernaturals are easy targets for anything nefarious. The police are far less likely to investigate as thoroughly. It could be anything. It doesn't necessarily mean the labs are opening again. I don't think I've heard of any vampires going missing, but I will ask," he added, sensing Harriet's unease still.

"Okay," Harriet was still feeling wobbly, so she took a large sip from her mug, glad Dan had insisted on leaving it there. "Okay, but you'll still check?"

"Of course I will."

Harriet and Simon talked for a few more minutes before Connor came back in the room.

"Okay, bye," She hung up. "What did Dan say?"

Connor sat on the end of the mattress, looking like the world was ending, although that could have been the hangover still.

"He said he hadn't heard of any cases, but he'd ask his mum to have an ask around. He said something about her being quite influential? Alpha Owens, I think her name is."

Harriet almost spat out her drink. "Alpha Owens?"

"I'm pretty sure that's what he said." Connor looked worried now, like he'd said something wrong.

"Alpha Owens is majorly influential. It's one of the biggest packs in Wales and Shropshire. I didn't realise Dan was one of her sons. Most of her children are high flying lawyers or doctors, or…" Harriet struggled to think of anymore ridiculously well paid jobs. "I think one of them is an actor. She's doing quite well actually. Maybe they just aim high and succeed." Harriet scoffed. Bloody overachievers, and there was her, with degrees in most subjects and still hadn't settled on a course of action.

"Dan runs a successful coffee shop chain," Connor said loyally. "He's doing very well for himself."

Harriet didn't argue. She apparently knew the Owens pack far less well than Connor, although she'd argue that Connor didn't actually know they were the Owens pack.

"I thought Dan had his own pack, but he said he's still in his mum's pack. I didn't want to say anything in case I came across as a—" he gestured, looking for the word.

"Uneducated human," Harriet suggested.

Connor clicked his fingers and pointed at her, "Yes!"

"I don't know much about werewolf packs. There's a brief chapter in Sabina's book. That's the extent, werewolves and vampires don't really share intimate details about biology and social etiquette." Harriet remembered meeting an interesting were in the late 1700s, but etiquette for most bipedals had changed since then. "From what I understand, packs are all based in family, but act like business. In the sense that Alpha Owens is your top man, and her pack is everyone. Your heads of department are her children, and they will each have their own pack, usually when they start a family, but also if they bite anyone. Anyone in their pack reports to their Alphas, but all Alphas report to their head, which in this case is Alpha Owens."

"So, anyone can be Alpha?"

"Yeah, you just have to be head of your little pack, within the context of the bigger pack. It's like in wolf packs in the wild, the heads of the pack are normally just the parents, Alpha is just a title to denote that."

"Okay, that makes sense." They both sat there in contemplative silence for a second. "Anyway, who were you on the phone with?"

"Simon. I was asking about any missing vamps. He hasn't heard anything, but he's going to have an ask around. Well, he's going to ask Sabina, that's his 'network', although he never admits it."

"Okay, so initial impression. No vamps and weres have gone missing, but definitely witches and maybe demons." Connor paused, "Maybe Mr Jones was kidnapped by whoever is kidnapping these people."

Harriet considered it, but it seemed like too much of a coincidence. "I don't think so. Besides, Mr Jones was kidnapped from his home."

"Were the witches kidnapped from the club?" Connor started. "I thought they had just visited the club before they went missing."

Harriet went to shoot it down, but realised that she couldn't say for sure. She sent a quick text to Alice.

Were witches kidnapped AT the club, or just scouted there?

"If they weren't kidnapped at the club, then Mr Jones could have just happened to have been kidnapped, separate to his dealings," Connor said.

"He'd have to be the unluckiest being alive if that were the case," Harriet said.

Dan came down the stairs carrying more food. "You're worried about the labs opening?" he asked Harriet.

Harriet nodded. "It was just a thought, if supernaturals are being kidnapped, but Simon is going to help check."

"I've got my mum asking as well, about weres. I haven't heard anything though, so I think it's okay. Did you get taken into one of the labs?" Dan asked quietly.

"Only briefly. It was about a month before they got shut down. I didn't have it as bad as some. Sabina spent a year in one, managed to survive, though. What about you, you must have been five, six?" she asked.

"Four," he said. "But I managed to avoid the labs." They'd only be open for about two years before Darrow had gained control and shut them down. It was the only pro-supernatural legislation he passed, although he had simply called it the 'Humanity Law', which often got referred to as the 'Human Bloody Decency' Law.

"My mum wasn't so lucky, was in there for months. It disrupted the entire pack hierarchy because there was a change in Alphas. Luckily, we made it through until she came back, but I know a lot of packs perished because of fighting within ranks."

"Humans," Harriet said with derision, and then a quick 'sorry' in Connor's direction, who made a noise Harriet interpreted as 'No, I agree'.

"So, what are we going to do about it?" Connor asked.

Harriet inhaled. Dan and Connor were both looking to her for direction, much like Simon and Cora once had, although she wasn't sure how she had ended up as unofficial leader. "I don't know about what we do if the labs are back, but we need to go back and have another, more sober look around that club."

If she had to be leader, she may as well act like she knew what she was doing. She was pretty sure that's all anyone was doing anyway.

Chapter Twelve

Harriet didn't think she'd ever spent this much time at the library, and she'd been a student who couldn't go out in sunlight for nearly 200 years. Harriet and Connor were once again back in the library, several days after their hungover discussion. This time they had brought Dan. Harriet wondered who was covering all of Dan's night shifts, and whether he'd told them the truth about why he had to change, that he was off investigating murder and kidnappings with a vampire and not quite human.

She was imagining Dan's grumpy personality having to deal with the bustle of daytime shifts at the coffee shop when Simon sat down with them.

"Okay, so technically I'm helping you out with research inquiries so I can talk while I'm not on break," Simon said.

Harriet wasn't sure why. He was the head librarian, and only answered to Sabina. He could probably spend all his time reading, leave it to the interns and wouldn't get told off, although he insisted he wasn't leaving his library in the hands of interns. 'Are you mad?' he'd said when she'd suggested it once, 'That's as good as burning it down'.

"So, I looked into any instance of vampires going missing post labs and I can't find anything. There was one who went missing and suspected burnt about 10 years ago but that was miles away. And a few dotted over the last couple years, again mostly suspected accidental burnings, one suspected hate crime and one that was found to have been one of the victims in a mass shooting, unrelated to supernatural status, just in the wrong place at the wrong time. Once the sun rose, his body was destroyed. It took months to identify him, which is why he was listed as missing." Simon concluded, putting a stack of papers in front of her, a collection of printed stats and newspaper articles. "None of them were within five miles of here, nor in any way associated with this bar of yours, apart from the fact they were vampires, there was no rhyme or reason to them."

"Okay, thank you for that," Harriet said, the heavy feeling in her stomach had eased somewhat, especially as Dan had informed her yesterday that similarly, there had been no suspicious werewolf disappearances in the last few years. The ones who had were attributed to hate crimes or pack disputes.

It looked like they were in the clear from labs.

"Hang on," Connor said, picking up a particular newspaper article. Harriet heart dropped, "How was he killed in a shooting? Cora said vampires can only be killed by a stake to the heart."

Simon let out a short laugh, and Harriet sighed. She was going to kill Cora. "Cora plays a game where she tries to get away with the biggest lie about vampires."

"Now, now, you both used to play it," Simon said. "Who was it that convinced that American soccer mum you could telepathically communicate with bats? I'm sure she freaked and reported it to the news."

Harriet rolled her eyes, "Yes but I stopped playing it because it led to so much misinformation." It had been her that convinced the soccer mum. She had reined champion for three years before Cora persuaded a man at a bus stop that her father was Dracula.

"So, it isn't a stake?" Connor asked.

"No," Harriet sighed, "As I said, vampires are built like humans. We've got tougher skin but anything damaging our internal organs is going to have the same effect. A stake to the heart will kill us, but so will a bullet."

"Why the stake lore then?" Dan asked this time.

"Hunters, way back in the day, used to convince the townspeople only a special stake that they had access to could kill vampires, so they could charge people to get rid of their vampire infestation. If the townspeople knew a particularly heavy rock to the head would have done the same trick, they could have done it themselves."

"Are you telling me that capitalism caused vampire lore?" Connor asked.

Harriet nodded, "And any misnomers from the mid-1800s onward was probably me and Cora."

Connor huffed, "Never trusting Cora again."

Harriet laughed, "The best way to get back at Cora is to play her at her own game. Tell her ridiculous human facts. It's been so long since she was one, she's probably forgotten."

Connor developed an evil glint in his eyes that caused Simon to give Harriet the most unimpressed look possible.

"Anyway," Simon said pointedly. "I have been digging deeper into the bar's history, and it's quite interesting." Simon pulled another pile of papers in front of him.

There was a pause, as if Simon were waiting for someone to ask him, 'What's interesting?'. Nothing came, so he continued.

"Basically, what it is, is that it has had several police cautions over the years for illegal activity."

Another pause for the expectant 'What activity?', and again silence.

Simon huffed, "It was implicated in drug trafficking, cocaine and other Class A drugs."

Harriet raised an impressed eyebrow at that. Usually the only illegal activity that happened at supernatural bars was importing high potency alcohol to get werewolves drunk, and questioning regarding the sourcing of large quantities of blood for vampires, Class A drugs was a new one.

"Convicted?" She asked.

Simon shook his head. "Although these charges have been brought up on multiple occasions, and one of the managers was charged and sentenced for possession of drugs and intent to sell. I think the club is a front for their drug trade. Also, rather interestingly, the owner and most of the managers are human."

That was unusual, as while most supernatural bars were run edging the line of illegal in where they sourced their stuff, not that there was a lot of choice. Every supernatural club Harriet had ever come across was run by supernaturals themselves.

"So, what does that mean?" Connor asked. "Why is the fact they do drugs important?"

"It means they're more likely to be inclined to do other illegal activities, like kidnapping," Dan realised. "You think the bar was helping whoever did this?"

"I still think it's this facility, even if it's not a lab. I reckon they're kidnapping these girls for something," Harriet said, "And wouldn't it be so much easier if the bar were on their side, throw in the fact that most of them disappeared there and the others might have. It just looks incredibly suspicious."

"Why do you think the facility is linked to the kidnappings?" Dan asked.

"This town had a population of what, 12,000? Murders and kidnapping just don't happen, and for both to be happening at the same time. I think it's all linked somehow. Mr Jones, Ms Pickett, the facility and the kidnapping, unless there's something in the water making people nefarious." Harriet was certain that there were far too many loose threads on this, tangled together and tugging out in different directions; you just needed to find the point they all led back to.

Connor and Dan only looked half convinced.

"Fine, we can treat Jones and Pickett as separate from the bar and kidnappings for now, but I bet we can find a link," Harriet said.

"Like this," Connor said, suddenly reaching for the pile of papers in front of Simon. Connor turned them and faced them towards him. "The logo of the damn place." He turned the papers to face Harriet and then Dan. "Do you remember the beer mats at the bar, they had the bar logo on them, right?"

"Yeah?" Harriet and Dan said.

"I saw some at Mr Jones' apartment. They were stacked on the TV stand. They must have gone the next time we were there because the TV and stand had both gone as well."

"That just proves a demon went to a demon and witches' bar. It's the only one in town," Dan said, "I'd be more surprised if he didn't go to it."

"No, I remember seeing some more on the kitchen table," Harriet said, she remembered thinking it was odd at the time, considering he not only physically couldn't drink, but also didn't even have drinks for friends coming round. Mr Jones was an introvert at heart, despite the fact he didn't have one, and he had no time for anyone who wasn't similarly interested in his favourite topics. Harriet didn't think he had any friends and he had certainly never mentioned anyone in his life.

So, why would a demon go to a bar, other than to meet up with friends? They certainly couldn't drown their troubles in drink, even if they had the functioning organs, demons couldn't get drunk.

"It seems an odd thing," she said to the table. "For a demon who can't drink to have that many beer mats, there was at least six on the table in the kitchen."

She looked to Connor, who scrunched up his face, "I didn't count but maybe 20 or 30. There were quite a few stacked up in multiple piles."

Even Dan frowned at that, "Okay, that is odd."

Harriet grinned. It was always nice to be proven right, even if it meant your English teacher may be mixed up in the kidnapping of nine underage girls. "I think it's time for another visit to Mr Jones' flat."

Simon scoffed, "You two practically live there, the amount of times you've been round."

"Third time's the charm," She argued.

"Oh my god," Connor said suddenly, apparently full of epiphanies today. "I've been a moron."

Harriet raised her eyebrow.

"Alice is a witch. She probably knows loads of covens round here."

"Yeah?" Harriet said, still not understanding Connor's point.

"So, she might be able to tell us more about Pickett and her coven. The more we know about what the hell she's up to with that USB the better. If Mr Jones is linked to the bar, Pickett probably is too," Connor said excitedly.

Harriet wasn't sure it called for that much enthusiasm. She doubted whatever Alice knew about Pickett's coven wasn't going to lead them to a startling break through about the USB stick. However, who was she to crush Connor's enthusiasm?

"Great, if you look into that, I'll go back to Jones' flat, hopefully it hasn't been completely cleared."

"I'm meeting Alice tomorrow, anyway. She said she'd help try and teach me magic." Connor looked inordinately pleased.

"I'll see if I can get a more complete list of everyone who has disappeared from the club, including demons," Dan offered.

"So that's settled. I'll go to Jones' flat. Connor will interrogate Alice during his Hogwarts night classes and Dan will compile a list of missing demons."

"And I will be staying out of trouble for plausible deniability when you all get arrested," Simon said, already collecting his sheets of paper to put away.

Harriet grinned, "Spoilsport."

Chapter Thirteen

Mr Jones' flat had been surprisingly worth the trip. Harriet thought most of it would have been cleared by now, and while most of the furniture and his belongings had gone, there were still a few beer mats hanging around. Harriet had been about to call the whole thing off and go home, after having spent nearly two hours checking every nook and cranny downstairs, checking for loose floorboards and drawers with hidden bottoms when she found a stack of beer mats in the first drawer that she looked in upstairs. Not hidden away, or even covered with anything, just sat in a desk drawer, waiting to be found. Well, waiting to be found by anyone willing to break in and rummage around.

She almost discarded them as useless, because who hid incriminating evidence inside a drawer that wasn't even locked? She'd only picked them up to give them a cursory glance over when she noticed it.

*

Harriet, Connor, and Dan regrouped at the coffee shop the next evening. Well, Harriet and Connor did. Dan was technically working, not that there was anyone else in the shop.

"Hey, why is there never anyone else in the coffeeshop when we're here?" Harriet asked. It had always been quiet in here. She had been curious about it in passing before, but not enough to ask the owner who she'd had an easy business relationship with. She knew Dan better now.

"You guys have a weird early evening lecture, and then nothing for the rest of the night. Most vampires have classes between 9PM and 1AM, and then they come in here, so you just miss the rush, as much as thirty odd vampires can be called a rush," Dan said.

"Huh, makes sense, I guess," Harriet said, "Although I kind of like the quiet. Means I normally get work done. Until you showed up," she said teasingly to Connor.

He laughed. "Yeah, yeah, you know this is more interesting than Ms Pickett's essay question."

Harriet agreed, "So what did Alice say when you saw her?"

"Not a lot," Connor sighed, "Just that Pickett comes from the Davies coven, bunch of very old-fashioned witches, unusually so and that their numbers are depleting because apparently their family has a high number of male witches and they keep kicking them out."

Harriet rolled her eyes, "Sounds about right."

"However," Connor said. "Alice was sceptical when I told her we thought Pickett was dodgy. She said no matter how ridiculous their traditions are, they're also old fashioned in the sense that they're highly moralistic and doubted they'd be interested in any financial gain as they're all from old money too."

"And yet, Pickett is a teacher," Harriet said, not willing to let this go. She was so sure everything was connected, although she doubted Alice was going to help with the USB stick.

"Maybe her family's wealth allowed her to pursue what she wanted to do," Dan countered.

"Torturing young minds," Connor said.

"Teaching English or researching. University lecturers do research as well, right?" Dan said.

"Yeah, which still makes me think she found something out about Jones' research, and she's selling it or something." Harriet took a vicious bite out of her muffin.

"Or," Connor said, looking like he couldn't believe what was about to come out of his mouth. "I mean, I'm always the first to hope Pickett will get fired because of being dirty, but what if—" he paused, took a deep breath, and said, "What if she's actually innocent?"

Harriet paused in her muffin attack, "You're suggesting Pickett is innocent? You?"

Connor nodded, "It was the way you said it then. She found out about Jones' research but what if she didn't sell it? What if she tried to follow it up and got caught up in whatever Mr Jones was in or whoever he was in deep with?"

"Maybe we should hunt down that barrel-chested man Pickett was talking with. He might be a werewolf," Connor said, suddenly grinning manically, "Dan, since we've dragged you down the rabbit hole anyway, what say you come and join us on a werewolf hunt?"

Dan rolled his eyes, "Sure, when?"

"I was going to drop my essay off tomorrow. We can hang back after class to do that and you can meet us, and we'll follow Pickett again," Connor said.

"Why are you submitting the essay so early?" Harriet said. It wasn't due for another week. Harriet hadn't even looked at it yet, hadn't since Mr Jones got shot.

Connor looked at her in horror, "Because it's due tomorrow?"

"What." Harriet felt the situation seriously enough to exclude the use of inflection.

"The essay is due tomorrow."

"I thought it was due on the 18th."

"Tomorrow is the 18th." Connor had the expression of a parent telling their child their pet had died. Dan had the expression that he heard this conversation at least five times a day. *It's his own fault*, Harriet thought, *he shouldn't have opened a university coffee shop*, her panicked brain finding it safer to run off on a tangent than face the reality that she had an essay due in less than 24 hours and she had vaguely forgotten the title of it.

She had done worse before, she'd written a rambling 2000-word essay in four hours and finished half an hour before it was due. She'd drank a lot of energy drinks and not enough blood, so the drink had been sat burning a hole in her stomach lining for hours. She'd had cramp for days and had to neck blood every few hours until it healed itself. She had no intention of going through that again.

"Right, well. I'm going to go and do this essay, I'll see you both tomorrow, and we'll follow Pickett and go from there."

"Oh!" Dan said. "Hang on." He half jogged round to the back of the counter. Harriet and Connor had slowly been migrating tables closer to the counter. They were practically sat on top of it at this point.

"I have a list of demons who've gone missing from the bar." He held out a napkin with six names scrawled on it.

"That was fast," Harriet marvelled. She was impressed. She'd messaged Alice the morning after they'd been to the bar and Harriet still hadn't had a definitive list. She got the feeling Alice had forgotten.

"I remembered Simon saying the owners of the bar were human. People are more willing to talk when they're frightened that you're going to bite their head off." Dan let out a small smile, "Stereotypes come in handy sometimes."

Harriet laughed, "I'll have to remember that in future." She could see why someone who didn't know Dan would be scared of him, he was easily six foot, broad and muscular. Also, he was incredibly hairy on his forearms and the visible bit of his chest at the v of his shirt. Harriet had read once that other men find it emasculating to be less hairy. She wondered briefly if that was why women shaved so much. As a vampire, her hair only grew when she she'd had enough blood to get her body functioning, and then it grew in minute stages over months, so she rarely needed to shave or have a haircut. She sometimes forgot most women did it on a regular basis.

"Harriet?" Connor said, pulling her out of her mental tangent.

"Mm?"

"The essay?" Connor prompted.

"Right, yes!" She said. She folded the napkin and put it in her pocket. "I'll see you both tomorrow!"

She started back to her flat, already trying to plan out her essay. In her haste, she forgot to update Connor and Dan about the beer mats she'd found.

*

Harriet managed to finish the essay by 8AM. She read it through one final time before double saving it, printing it out and placing it carefully on top of her bag, ready to take with her.

She set her alarm, and fell asleep on top of her duvet, which was still littered with journal articles and highlighters.

*

She sat yawning in Pickett's class, waiting for the few stragglers to file in. She was surprised anyone would dare, they'd have to know what Ms Pickett was like by now. If you dared turn up late to her class, she'd verbally take you down in front of the entire class, before calling on you for every question and find pleasure in mocking your incorrect answers. She would also give you this shrewd look when you took your first step across the doorway any later than a second

84

past the hour, like she was mental filing your appearance away for a voodoo doll. Harriet may be basing that last one on stereotype, she didn't actually believe witches used voodoo. Mostly. The only time she had was briefly, the first and only time she'd been late to one of Ms Pickett's lectures, and Pickett had given her that exact look.

Harriet looked at the clock. It hit the hour and Connor still wasn't there. She frowned. Connor was never late; he too had a healthy respect for Ms Pickett's voodoo glare.

Harriet slyly took her phone out of her pocket and messaged Connor:

Where are you? Pickett is gonna do the voodoo face.

Harriet had not received a reply in 10 minutes, and she was checking her phone every time Pickett turned her gaze elsewhere. Pickett had the same outlook on phones in the classroom as a vampire in a sunbed; namely that they shouldn't be there, and they were likely to die as a result of using it.

After almost 20 minutes, she received a reply:

Sorry, not feeling well. Have given Dan my essay, can you hand it in please?

Harriet frowned, she texted back an affirmation, and put her phone back in her pocket for the first time in 20 minutes.

She found the lecture dragged without someone to exchange sidelong glances with every time Pickett was particularly boring or said something incredibly hypocritical.

She'd once accused Mr Belani of marking easy on some of his student's papers and had repeatedly told the class they wouldn't get special treatment in her class. Which was ridiculous, while she was saying this, Harriet saw her overlook a couple of witches whispering and showing each other memes on their phones.

By the time Pickett finished Harriet realised she hadn't taken a word in of that entire lecture and was going to have to go through the lecture online at some point, because she was sure it covered the exam they had in a month before they broke up for Christmas, and she was going to have to fill Connor in on what he missed.

"Remember, today is the deadline for your essays, please drop your printed essays into this box before you leave." She placed a box on her desk and dismissed the class.

Harriet shuffled in line. Being sat at the back of the class meant she was at the back of the line for dropping in her essay.

By the time she reached the front of the line, and was the last person in the room, except Pickett, she could see Dan hovering by the door, so she waved him in.

"Ms Pickett, Connor's ill today, so Dan is dropping his essay off," she explained, mostly because Ms Pickett looked briefly terrified when she saw Dan in the doorway.

"Oh yes, of course. Mr Manning emailed me earlier to inform me. Apologies," she directed to Dan, "I thought you were someone else."

Ms Pickett grabbed the essay box and walked over towards Dan for him to drop Connor's essay into. Harriet couldn't be sure but she thought there was a hint of a blush on Ms Pickett's cheeks. As soon as he had done so, she grabbed her things and left. Whoever she had mistaken Dan for had got her in a flurry.

"She's the one who doesn't like Connor because she thinks he's human?" Dan asked, watching where Ms Pickett had just left.

"Yeah, come on, we should follow her, see if she's still meeting the burly dude. I wonder if that's who she thought you were?" Harriet said, starting off out the English building.

"Probably." Harriet could almost hear the eye roll in Dan's voice, without needing to turn and check. "Looks like a werewolf, has to be involved in dodgy stuff," Dan muttered to himself.

They made their way back out of the English block and followed the retreating figure of Ms Pickett towards the psychology building. Partway round, Harriet directed Dan to follow her round the back of the building, so they could sneak up the side without being seen.

They crouched down in the same spot that she and Connor had been previously.

Ms Pickett once again met with the burly man in the middle of the square. Harriet eyed them more closely this time, trying to work out what they were saying. They were so far away she couldn't get anything more than the odd word from lip reading, Dan was straining his head closer to them. Maybe he was able to hear what they were saying.

Once again, Ms Pickett handed over a USB drive, and the man handed over a piece of paper. This time, however, Harriet recognised the USB as Ms Pickett's own USB stick. Harriet had noticed she always had two, one for university work and one for personal use; the personal use one was purple, and Harriet was fairly sure it was the one being handed over.

Which meant there had to be a meetup to give her back her USB at some point, unless she was continually buying new ones, which seemed wasteful.

They both headed off in separate directions once the exchange had been made, and as soon as she figured they were out of earshot, she turned to Dan, "What were they saying?"

"They didn't say much. He said no more than 'the 25th', which is what, a week today? Probably meaning their next meet up if you said they last one was also after class. Maybe they do it every week."

"What did she say?" Harriet asked, filing that information away for later, although she'd figured they probably had a semi regular schedule.

"She said thank you when he handed her the paper, and when she handed him the USB, she nodded to it, and said, 'What are you using him for?'. I'm assuming she meant Mr Jones."

"Mm," Harriet said. She thought back to the beer mats and a sudden, terrifying chill went through her.

"What else?" Dan said, taking her silence as doubt. "You reckon it's to do with his research?" Dan asked. Harriet just shrugged.

"Also," Dan said, as if just remembering. "He's not a werewolf."

"Hm?"

"The-burly, er dude," he said awkwardly, the words sounding too colloquial in his mouth. "He's not a werewolf." He hesitated, "I don't mean to speculate, but some human groups use werewolves as bouncers because then humans make less trouble, but because they don't want to actually employ any supernaturals, they get humans that are muscled and hairy, who everyone assumes are werewolves and they rely completely on stereotype alone."

"Damn, I suppose it might come in handy for them, but that must suck."

Dan hummed his agreement, "As I said, it can come in handy sometimes. I got the information from the club because they were basing what I'd do off stereotype. My sister uses it to her advantage, although in a different way," he said.

"Your sister Madison?" Harriet asked, wondering what different way there was.

Dan nodded, "Yeah but most of my family are dark haired and well-muscled, including all my sisters, but Madison, my little sister, is the opposite. Blonde and very slim, she gets it from somewhere on dad's side of the family, but it works in her favour. You'd think she was a witch if you didn't know better. Means when some jackass tries to grab her or try something, he gets a mighty shock when she gets out the claws and fangs."

"Huh, suppose I'd never thought of it like that."

"Neither had Madison at first. She was always cut up about the way she looked, but then she discovered by human beauty standards she was gorgeous and has been fully taking advantage of the fact people not only trust her because she's pretty but also because they don't realise she's a werewolf." Dan had the tone of an older brother down to pat, protective yet proud.

There was a noise on the courtyard that drew both Harriet and Dan's attention.

"Is someone there?" Harriet whispered. Dan nodded, tilting his head to hear better.

"How long have they been there?" Harriet's heart had picked up in fear. She knew she shouldn't have had the extra cup of blood, but she'd needed waking up after her late morning writing spree.

"Don't know," Dan said, his voice no more than a breath. "I wasn't actively listening. I have to tune it out sometimes, otherwise I'd go mad."

Harriet huffed. Although she supposed that was fair, if you had to hear every minute whisper and quiet noise within a room's span on top of your standard noise, it would probably end up quite deafening.

During his listening, Dan had slowly been following the noise round with his head, until much to Harriet horror, he continued turning until he was facing directly behind them.

Where Ms Pickett stood in fine fury.

*

Harriet was going to die. She was going to get murdered by her substitute teacher because she was investigating the murder of her normal teacher, along

88

with the grumpy werewolf who owned the coffee shop who she hadn't properly known until a month ago. Now, they were about to die together.

When she'd been told at freshers that everybody was in the same boat at university, she didn't quite think that held true.

She mentally apologised to the humans she'd yelled at for their prejudiced thoughts about how wild supernatural universities must be. Although statistically speaking, if you took a million human universities, surely the same scenario would play out to more or less the same effect. She hoped so, at any rate, and spared a thought for the human versions of her and Dan who were stood, stock still in terror at their human Ms Pickett.

"What," the supernatural Ms Pickett hissed, "the hell do you think you're doing?" Her fists were clenched, as if she were holding herself back from casting a rather nasty spell on them.

In fact, as human Harriet and Dan weren't in danger of being magical beaten up, she had no sympathy for them.

"We know what you're doing." Harriet's words might have sounded brave in her head, had she actually thought about them before they left her mouth. She didn't, though, and so they sounded timid and more garbled than intended.

"And what precisely do you think I'm doing?" she asked.

"You found out Mr Jones was in deep with some dodgy people. It's something to do with his research, isn't it, and what? You tried to blackmail him, or did you get caught up in it too?" Harriet figured she may as well go for it; she was about to die at any second.

Simon always did say her curiosity would get her killed one day, although he was probably imagining she was going to stick her head in a wind turbine or something equally stupid.

"Research?" she scoffed, as it she couldn't help herself. Harriet realised she'd never seen Ms Pickett look so dishevelled before. Her tight bun had several scraggly fly aways that were now framing her face, which looked tired and heavy with lines in the low light.

"It's not research?" she guessed. "What is it?"

Ms Pickett was already shaking her head. "Stop here, don't go looking any further. That's what I did and look where it got me." She gestured to where she and the burly man had been standing.

"So, you what? Noticed Mr Jones acting suspicious, and decided to check it out?"

Ms Pickett pursed her lips. "No, I was here late one evening. I'd sat in on a lecture from Mr Jones. He was thinking of transferring, so I was to take over his class. Anyway, I went to ask him something afterwards, but he'd gone. I found him here talking to that man when I was heading for the car park."

Harriet remembered Ms Pickett sitting in on the lecture, but she hadn't known it was because Mr Jones was planning to leave.

"And you thought it was dodgy?" Dan prompted in the face of Harriet's silence.

"No, I haven't met every lecturer here, and it's not unusual for some to stay late. I mentioned it in passing to him the next day, asked if the man was a new professor, but Mr Jones was evasive about it. He sounded panicked." She hesitated over the last word. "It was frantic enough that it made me believe the transfer had more to do with moving than the increased salary."

"So, you investigated?" Harriet asked, wondering when Ms Pickett was going to put a stop to the questioning.

"I inquired," she said pointedly. "It was enough to get the attention of the man you saw tonight."

Dan nodded like Ms Pickett had finished speaking. She certainly had the same look on her face as when she'd gotten fed up answering questions in class. Harriet wasn't ready to let this go yet, so she pulled out her final hand.

"The USB stick. Was it the list of names, kidnapping victims, or was it the next lot who are about to disappear?" She tried to get it out confidently, with a casual air that suggested she'd known all along. Technically, she'd known since she found the stack of beer mats at Mr Jones' flat. Each one with a different name and phone number on, all corresponding to a kidnapping victim, including some that weren't on Harriet's list. She had been praying there was an alternative answer.

Ms Pickett's mouth opened slightly in shock, which Harriet figured for the woman was probably gaping.

"How do you—"

"You and Mr Jones gave that man the names of young witches for them to kidnap?" she asked, the words feeling as though they were dripping from her mouth. She was half tempted to wipe her mouth with her sleeve, just to get rid of the awful feeling.

From the corner of her eye, Harriet noticed Dan giving her a wide-eyed look.

"No!" Ms Pickett cried. "Certainly not. I—" She hesitated, "I suppose it's not much better. I gave them the names of demons. I did the best I could do, given the circumstances," she insisted, more to herself.

"And what circumstances were those?" Dan beat Harriet to it. He sounded furious.

"I only gave them the names of criminals. Unfortunately I don't know very many of those, despite what a small town it is, so I had to resort to morally repugnant characters," she defended herself, it seemed, mostly out of habit, knowing full well no one, including herself, was believing her.

"So, people who you thought were criminals and people you thought were just a bit mean."

"I only had a week to find three people. Every week, another three people, it's incessant."

"Mr Jones used the bar Magic to pick up girls, mostly underage, who'd fallen out with their families, and used them," Harriet said, Ms Pickett looked for a second like she was about to cry, before her eyes steeled.

"If the alternative was anything like mine, I'm not surprised."

"What was your alternative?" Harriet asked. "Money?"

For a prim and proper witch, Ms Pickett gave the highest standard of 'Bitch, please' looks that Harriet had ever received.

"They paid us, but only enough so if they got busted, it would look like we were willing accomplices. No, the real incentive was if we 'volunteered' others, we wouldn't get taken ourselves." Ms Pickett was shaking as her hand tried to tuck a strand of hair behind her ear.

"Taken where?" Harriet whispered, knowing already in her gut the words before Ms Pickett spoke them.

"They've opened another lab, like the ones after the reveal," Ms Pickett said. "You don't understand what they were like. I was there for almost a year, and I was one of the only witches they had, which meant their 'curiosity' wasn't even spread over a group of us." Ms Pickett had given up with the strand of hair. Her hands were shaking too badly, and she let her arms drop, defeated, to her sides.

"My mum was in those labs for almost a year," Dan said, with steel in his voice. Harriet noticed his eyes were red rimmed. "And not once did she sell out a single member of our pack, or anyone else's."

Harriet rested a hand on Dan's shoulder, and quietly added, "You forget I'm four hundred and fifty years old. I was in those labs. I've been in several labs over my time, but those after the reveal were the worst. I *know* what they were like."

"Then you know why I had to do it," Ms Pickett said.

Harriet thought about it genuinely. They had rounded up any supernatural they could find, even people they only thought were supernatural. She and Simon had been taken from their university, paraded past any human staff or students who'd been there late enough and taken into the labs. It was the only time she'd been truly thankful of Cora's decision to go out to work.

She and Simon had only seen each other in passing for the few months they'd both been in the lab, but it had always been a relief to see the other, just to know they were still alive. There had been test on how quickly a vampire's internal organs would shut down without blood, and the strength of sunlight needed to disintegrate a vampire. Harriet remembered faces disappearing from the mess hall, never to be seen again.

And she knew, without a doubt, she would never want to inflict that on anyone.

"No. I couldn't. Not after living through it myself. I couldn't knowingly put anyone else through that experience," Harriet said.

Ms Pickett scoffed, becoming less well put together throughout the course of the conversation. "You both stand there so high and mighty about it, but if you were in my shoes, actually given the choice, faceless people over yourself, no one knowing it was you, it's instinctual, I know you'd do the same as me."

Harriet wondered if she would. People said they wouldn't do a lot of things, but put in the situation without other's judgement, most end up doing things they never thought they would.

Harriet's phone started ringing. She ignored it. "Is that everything you know? Do you know where the facility is?"

Ms Pickett shook her head. "All I know is that I'm meant to meet here once a week with at least three names, and I get a check, and excused from being taken. I know Mr Jones had the same deal. Look, can I go?"

"You think we're going to let you go after what you've told us?" Dan said incredulously.

"You have to," Pickett implored, "They shot Mr Jones as a warning when he threatened to go to the police. Now, he's disappeared too. I won't heal from bullet hole."

Dan looked as if he were about to say 'Good', when Harriet phone started ringing again.

"Hello?" She picked it up without checking who it was.

"Oh my god, Harriet, thank god you picked up!" Alice's panicked voice came through the phone. Harriet saw Dan turn his head to listen to the conversation.

"What's wrong?" Harriet asked.

"Me and Connor thought we'd go back to the club to have a scout around. We thought it'd look less suspicious without a vamp and were. That's why he told you he was ill, but—"

Alice sounded close to tears, and Harriet's stomach dropped out, "Alice, what happened?"

"I can't find Connor. I think someone's taken him."

Chapter Fourteen

Harriet had been in a car with Dan on a few occasions now, and she'd never once feared for her life like she did now.

He screeched round corners and ran several red lights. When he finally pulled up outside the club, it was with a final sudden break that flung Harriet forward in her seat so hard it knocked the air out of her lungs. He didn't bother properly parking, just left the car parked where it was, at a drastic angle to the pavement. Although Harriet suspected if she'd been driving, she would have done a similar thing.

They both rushed out, and found Alice almost immediately stood outside with Petal. Alice looked timid for the first time. She was still in her usual 50s style dress, make up and heels, this time all in various shades of dark blue, but she looked unsure of herself for the first time. Her arms were wrapped around her body and she was shivering in the cold night air.

Harriet took off her jacket and flung it around Alice's shoulders. Harriet noticed Alice's mascara had run, little black tracks down her cheeks. She looked like the young girl she was.

"Hey," Harriet said softly. "What happened?" Her hands were still resting lightly on Alice's shoulders. She had fully prepared to come here and yell at Alice for her and Connor wandering off, and she could feel Dan's tense form stood next to her, like he still wanted to yell. Harriet found herself incapable, though; the sight of Alice's young-looking face just made her think of what all the other poor girls who'd been kidnapped were going through, what Connor might now be going through.

"We came here to check out the club again, but I told Connor that no one was going to tell us anything if we had other supernaturals with us. They especially weren't going to be interested in taking us to the facility if we did," Alice mumbled.

"Hang on," Harriet said, and she felt Dan simultaneously tense up next to her again.

"You were *trying* to get kidnapped?" Dan said, his voice loud enough to make several heads near them turn.

Harriet half-heartedly shushed him. She was also fuming about this new revelation.

"No, not—we just wanted to find out who was taking people. I didn't mean to get him kidnapped."

"How do you know he got kidnapped? Are you sure he's not in the bathroom?" Dan said hopefully.

Alice glared at Dan. If looks could kill, Dan would be deader than Dracula in daylight. "I'm blind, not a moron. His aura's not here."

Dan frowned.

"Look," Harriet said, tucking Alice under her arm when she shivered. It was slightly difficult considering Alice was taller than her, especially in her heels. Petal whined miserably at Alice feet; even she looked downtrodden. "We're gonna go in. Dan is going to threaten management until they show us the CCTV files and find out who kidnapped Connor, and then we're going to find him."

"We need to do it quickly, though," Dan said.

"Yes, we—we found out a bit more about the research facility." Harriet didn't know whether telling Alice now about the labs was going to spiral her about losing Connor. "They've been getting people like Mr Jones and Ms Pickett to give them the names of supernaturals and then kidnapping them into the labs, like the ones they had about 20 years ago."

Alice's large watery eyes looked between Harriet and Dan, "My mum said those things were horrible, that they weren't proper labs."

"They were horrible. Was your mum in one?" Harriet asked.

Alice shook her head, "No, none of my coven were, but she said she heard horror stories about what went on in them."

"We cornered Ms Pickett and she told us, and there were some incriminating beer mats with the kidnappees' names and numbers on them in Mr Jones' flat."

"Do you think, Connor said Ms Pickett never liked him. Did she give his name?" Alice asked.

"No," Harriet and Dan said. Dan had all but pinned Ms Pickett to the side of the psychology building, demanding to know if Connor's name had been on the USB, to which Ms Pickett had looked incredibly confused and said 'Connor?

Connor Manning? He's human, why would I give his name?'. Harriet and Dan had both deemed her to be honestly confused and had run off to Dan's car.

"Ms Pickett thinks he's human. That's why she doesn't like him," Harriet explained.

"Oh," Alice sniffed. "Right," she said, gathering herself up, wiping ineffectively at her run make up. "I'm ready to go back in." She squared her shoulders, and looked ready to murder the man on the door. All Harriet and Dan could do was trail after her.

"I need to go back in," she said, ignoring the people lined up waiting.

"There's a queue," the bouncer said, uninterestedly.

"I was in there before. I only stepped out because I couldn't find my friend. I thought he'd be out here. I'm blind, you see, and I was just scared." Tears were welling up in Alice's eyes again. Harriet couldn't tell if it was good acting, or whether Alice was frustrated and already upset.

"I—fine," the bouncer said, eyeing the judgmental stares of other clubbers, no one wanting to be accused of discriminating against a blind person. "You can go in." Alice and Harriet made their way past the bouncer, but he put an arm across before Dan could step passed, "Only one non magic using guest per magic user, I'm afraid."

"But they're here to help me find my friend. He's a magic user. He was with me earlier."

"Sorry," the bouncer said unapologetically. Apparently having let the blind person in was enough preferential treatment in his book.

"Please," Alice's lower lip wobbled, and as if on cue, Petal whined. Several drunken people in the queue aww'd.

The bouncer opened his mouth as if he were about to let Dan past, until he looked at Dan properly, and suddenly said, "Hey, you're that were who terrorised management the other day. I've been told not to let you in again."

Dan looked mortified, and Alice swore quickly under her breath, before dragging Harriet in through the front doors before the bouncer could stop them.

"What are we going to do now?" Harriet asked, when they stopped at the bar. "Dan can't intimidate them into telling us when he's stuck outside."

"We're going to wing it," Alice said very confidently for someone who didn't look very confident at all.

In fact, they must have made quite the pair; Alice in her dress with a jacket over the top and smudged makeup, and Harriet in her jeans and T-shirt, looking exactly like she'd just come from a lecture, both illuminated by strobe lights. Stood by the bar in a nightclub, with a guide dog sat patiently at their feet.

"I need a drink first," Alice said.

"No. No drinking this time. We need to be completely sober. Let's see what the barman knows." Harriet flagged down one of the barmen. He was a pleasant looking man, slightly chubby with wild brown hair.

"Hello there, ladies. What can I get you?"

"Hi," Harriet slurred her voice slightly, and leant too heavily on the bar. "M'looking for my friend, he's tallish." She raised her hand in approximate Connor height. "He got big brown eyes, like big puppy dog eyes, and has dark brown hair in a big…" she tried to gesture to what Connor's hair quiff normally looked like, "…thing, but the sides are shaved, and—and he's," she looked at Alice for help before realising Alice wasn't going to be able to help with a physical description, "he's thin, young looking."

"He's a chatty bloke," Alice added, "Very excited. I think he was talking to someone at the bar."

"Is he the type to order cocktails?" the barman asked.

Harriet and Alice nodded. "And asked for extra cherries and umbrellas in it," Alice added.

"Yeah, I think I did see him. He was talking at the bar with a bloke for a bit. Not sure where he went after that, though."

"What did the guy look like? The one he was talking to?" Harriet asked.

The barman blew his cheeks out in thought. It made him look like a hamster. "Middle age bloke, beard, got a bit of a beer belly, um, think he was Scottish, he sounded it when he ordered."

Harriet sighed, "Thanks," she said, forgetting to act drunk, and the barman gave her a weird look. "Duuuude!" she cheered, making finger guns at him.

"I can ask the manager if you like?" he said, laughing at her drunken antics.

"Oh my god, would you? Thank you," she said, drawing out the *A* in thank. He disappeared back behind the bar.

A slimy looking man appeared along with the barman, who'd given them a thumbs up, mouthed 'manager' and pointed at the guy in front of them, before turning and serving someone at the other end of the bar.

"Hello there. I heard you've lost your friend," the man said. His smile was so greasy Harriet felt the need to wash herself when he grinned at her.

"Yeah, the barman said he was talking to a Scottish guy at the bar, and now he's vanished. We want to check the CCTV to see where he went," Harriet said, having given up the pretence of being wasted.

"I'm afraid I can't let you into the office for the CCTV, but I did see your friend. I believe the Scottish man offered him a drink and he declined, after that he started talking with a blonde girl at the bar, who he left with shortly after. He probably forgot to tell you," the manager smiled sickeningly at them. "Anything else?"

Harriet pursed her lips. There was going to be no persuading this man to let them have access to the CCTV footage.

"Nope," she smiled widely, her sharpened fangs on display. The manager's smile faltered somewhat and he stood up from his previous position of leaning on the bar.

"Yes, well, have a lovely evening then, ladies."

"Oh," Harriet called his attention back, stood on her tip toes and leaned as far as she could over the bar, "If I find my friend has been harmed, and you had any knowledge of any *kidnappings*," she emphasised the word by lingering over it, "I will not hesitate to seek any kind of justice I see fit." She grinned widely again, which was more baring her teeth than smiling, but it unnerved the man just the same, and she dug her fingernails into his arm, which he'd stupidly left resting on the bar. She saw him wince and was glad she hadn't had time to trim her nails recently.

"Goodnight," she said, before releasing him, linking her arm with Alice's and walking out of the nightclub.

*

"He said Connor left with some blonde woman, which he wouldn't do. He wouldn't leave the case, and he certainly wouldn't leave Alice." Harriet said, finishing filling Dan in on what had happened when they got back outside. The bouncer was giving the three of them sidelong glances from his position in front of the door.

"Yeah," Alice agreed. "Also because he's into guys, but totally because he wouldn't slack off either."

"He's into men?" Dan asked in interest. Harriet elbowed him to get back on track, but she definitely couldn't say she was surprised.

Alice hummed, "I mean, he never explicitly said but I could just tell, he—"

"What, was it in his aura?" Dan asked.

"No," Alice said. "He kept flirting with the guy behind the bar."

Harriet huffed, "Anyway, we know the manager was lying, but he seemed very keen to downplay what the barman said about a Scottish man, so I think that's our next lead."

"Just 'a Scottish man'?" Dan asked. "That's all we have to go on?"

"He also said he was potbellied and middle aged, which mostly rules out demons. They're all gorgeous and young." What was the point of being able to create your own body if it wasn't exactly to your own specification? It was why so many models and movie stars were demons. Plus, they never aged.

"Also, unlikely to be a witch, if he's male. I mean it's a possibility, but no coven of his generation would have kept him, and there were even fewer male witches 50 years ago," Alice said.

Harriet had read about that once. There was a spike in male witches about 20 years ago. They were still in the minority but before that they'd been the odd one in a couple hundred thousand. Now, it was resting more at one in a thousand. Some people thought it was due to something that had happened at the labs, some genetic tweaking. Others believed it was because male witches became more accepted socially and so more covens kept them and trained them, and so more appeared on the census.

"Either way," Dan argued. "Even if we've ruled out witch and demon, he could be anyone. I think we need to go to the police."

Harriet and Alice sighed.

Dan was right. They were going to have to go to the police.

*

The police station was busy, and the lady at the front desk was tired, and no doubt overworked. Although Harriet didn't appreciate it when she took one look at the clearly vampire, werewolf, and crying young girl, and visibly rolled her eyes.

She was human, as far as Harriet could tell, but unlike universities, there were not separate police stations for the supernatural. Police stations were not discriminatory, however, she suspected they saw the most stereotypical side of them all, vampires who still illegally hunted their victims, werewolves involved in bar brawls, and witches caught in inter-coven spell crossfire. They couldn't have a good impression of them.

Although the officers like the one who had accused Mr Jones of possession annoyed her, the ones who looked supernaturals like they were all criminal time bombs just waiting to commit felonies.

"Our friend has been kidnapped," Harriet said bluntly, trying to get the woman's attention. Her name tag said 'Susan'.

The woman raised an eyebrow. "An officer will be with you shortly, if you'll take a seat." She pointed to several incredibly vandalised seats. Harriet figured the worst chairs in the station got given to the waiting room, so the officers didn't have to sit on them.

"I would like to talk to Officer Wellard and Officer Sanwell they worked on Mr Jones' case. He was a demon who got shot on a university campus. I think the two might be related."

Susan raised her other eyebrow, but gave a vague nod, and then pointed again to the seating provided.

They sat down.

*

It took 45 minutes for an officer to get to them. Harriet supposed it was a busy night, human and supernatural wise. The officer who saw them introduced himself as Officer Jeffords, but call me, Ben looked about twelve, and this was possibly his first assigned case.

"All right, *Ben*," Dan said, with the tone of someone who'd been sat on an uncomfortable chair for the best part of an hour and wasn't happy about it. "Our friend has been kidnapped, and the longer we wait here, the longer his kidnappers have to get away. We specifically requested two officers," he looked at Harriet, who interjected 'Wellard and Sanwell,' Dan continued, "Because we think it relates to a case they were put on just over a month ago. So, *Ben* can you tell me what you're going to do."

Dan was livid. Harriet didn't know how much was being exaggerated to scare the probably human police officer, but Dan looked downright terrifying, looming particularly well over Ben, who was shorter than him by a good three or four inches.

"I, um, I don't know if Officer Wellard and Sanwell are on duty this evening. If you're happy for me to take your statement, however—"

"Oh, but we're not, *Ben*," Harriet joined in, grinning wildly to showed off her teeth for the second time this evening, hoping it would have the same effect as previously. It did.

"I can go and check if they're in—" he said, already half turned towards the door. Dan gave him a pointed look, and Ben hurried off down the corridor.

"That was a bit harsh," Alice pointed out. "Poor man was terrified, even I could sense it."

Dan shrugged, although Alice didn't see. "Found it's the best way to get things done. Mum's all about the politics and keeping people happy. I much prefer the direct approach. I find if you lay everything out for people, they respond much quicker."

"I'm sure the glaring helps more," Harriet said, and Alice snorted.

He turned back towards the door as he heard the approach of Ben. A few seconds later, Harriet and Alice heard two sets of footsteps coming down the corridor.

Ben came back through the doors, this time accompanied by Officer Wellard. Harriet was thankful it was him and not the human officer. Harriet remembered he'd accused Mr Jones of demonic possession, even though the evidence against that was glaring him in the face, in the form of the hole in Mr Jones' forehead.

"I see you're not happy with Officer Jeffords taking your statement. Can I ask why?" Wellard was as good at professional looming as Dan was menacing looming.

"We believe our friend's kidnapping is related to a case that you were working on," Dan said. Harriet was glad he was taking the initiative and talking to the police. Harriet always felt vaguely guilty and was sure if she was put under interrogation, she would admit to crimes she'd never committed.

Police freaked her out for some reason.

Wellard sighed, "Right, come on through then and I'll take your statements."

He took them through to a small, private room that looked like a small conference room. Harriet was just glad it wasn't an interrogation room.

He asked Dan to take him through the whole story, but Dan faltered. "Um, I actually wasn't there for the bit with Mr Jones." He looked towards Harriet.

Harriet sighed, and went from when Mr Jones got shot, Ms Pickett and what she and Connor saw. She mentioned going to Mr Jones' house and finding the letter, although she did say the door had been ajar, rather than telling the police officer they'd broken in. Wellard gave her a shrewd look but didn't stop her. She said about the second visit to Mr Jones' flat and him getting kidnapped, going to Alice and finding out about the witch kidnappings, the first visit to the club, the list of demons that had been kidnapped, the third visit to Mr Jones' flat. Even Ben was looking suspicious at how often Mr Jones left his front door ajar now. Harriet finally finished with what Ms Pickett had told them earlier about the labs, and then their rush to the club to find Connor gone.

"And the manager tried to cover it up by telling us that Connor had left with a blonde woman, but he wouldn't do that."

"And wouldn't leave Alice on her own, especially when they were investigating," Dan interjected.

"Exactly, so we think the manager was trying to deflect focus from whoever this Scottish guy is," Harriet finished. The whole thing had taken about half an hour to tell. Harriet wasn't surprised she'd forgotten about her essay; she couldn't believe how much they'd actually gotten up to in the last month.

"Which manager was it at the club? Do you know?" Ben asked, who had been taking notes on her entire piece.

"He didn't give his name, but he looked like a creepy, slimy character," Harriet said.

"Oh! I know the one. It'll be Creepy Jerry," Ben said, mouthing the words 'Creepy Jerry' as he wrote them.

Wellard closed his eyes briefly and took a deep breath, as if trying to resist the urge to hit Ben will a rolled-up newspaper. Harriet tried not to smile.

"Right, and why did you not come to the police with any of this information sooner?" Wellard asked.

"Well—" Harriet was trying to think of how to word 'We thought you were incompetent and prejudiced' in a way that wouldn't be offensive. Alice beat her to it.

"You had the investigation of Mr Jones' shooting, and you've been around the club because it was linked to the kidnapping, and you still haven't turned anything up. Forgive us if we were sceptical," Alice said.

Harriet bit her lip.

Wellard did not look impressed. "I cannot discuss ongoing investigations with civilians, but we have other sources of information, don't worry. The cases will be solved. Thank you for your time and information. I will disclose it with the respective main investigators on the cases. Now, if you will excuse me." He went to stand up.

"Hang on. What about Connor? Are you going to help us find him?" Dan said angrily.

"We will not be *helping* you with anything. We will be investigating, and you are not to join in," Wellard said, turning back to face Dan. "Your friend, Connor, hasn't been missing for 48 hours yet and you have no evidence of kidnapping. He might have simply gone home with someone from the bar. When 48 hours have passed, come back in and Officer Jeffords will fill out a missing persons form." Wellard turned and left.

Before the door had fully shut, Harriet loudly said, "You can report someone missing if you have probable cause to think they're missing!" knowing full well the werewolf would be able to hear her.

Ben smiled ruefully, "A lot of people say that, but it's not his fault. It's just procedure."

"He could be less mean about it," Alice insisted. Ben tactfully said nothing.

"I will see you all in 48 hours," Ben said, before exiting the room.

Harriet guessed they were to see themselves out then. In her head, she viciously called them every insult she could think of, before cathartically slamming the door shut on her way out.

They happened to bump back into Wellard again on their way out, or rather, Wellard heard them angrily muttering about how useless police were and how they should have just sorted it themselves and he approached them.

"Look," he said, pulling himself up to full height, and possible authority. "I know it can be an unpleasant thought, but you have to sit tight and let us do our jobs, and if I catch any of you around the Hampstead Estate, I will not hesitate to put you under house arrest. Now, you might want to get back quickly. Sunrise is in a few hours." He directed the last bit to Harriet.

"Yes, Officer," she said mulishly.

As soon as they got outside, Harriet grinned. "Okay, who knows where the Hampstead Estate is?"

Chapter Fifteen

The Hampstead Estate was almost not in town, it bordered between their town Clochcryn and the next town over, Llancallwen. It was also a very non-descript direction. The Hampstead Estate covered a lot of land, including the actual estate of council flats, the yard that came with it, which was mostly an acting graveyard for litter and deflated footballs. It also came with a plot of land set slightly further back from the main road with a building that had to be the facility.

It was tall and looked like a block of office flats. It could have easily been the building on the logo from the letter Mr Jones received. It also had fencing around the perimeter and an operator booth outside the gates for cars to drive up to. It also, in the clincher of Ominous Government Building Clichés, had security men posted sporadically around the fence, which was always the staple of a dodgy building in Harriet's opinion. The lights were still on in the building, and it looked like it was still up and running at two in the morning.

Unfortunately, they'd had to wait until the next evening to go as by the time they'd gotten back from the police station, it was nearing sunrise; Harriet had tried to persuade them to go on without her, but Dan and Alice both insisted they needed to sleep as they'd both been awake for nearing the 24-hour mark.

They'd also been under the mistaken impression that the place would be easier to scope out at night because it would have shut down for the evening. Apparently, there really was no rest for the wicked, as there had been multiple cars going in and out over the last several hours.

"What do you reckon they're up to?" Alice asked.

"They're trying to open the labs again," Harriet muttered, angry at Connor and Alice for putting him in such a dangerous position. She supposed neither of them had ever truly experienced the labs or even had anyone close to them experience it, like Dan.

"No. I mean why. From our point of view, the labs were horrific, but for them, why open the labs? What more knowledge can be gained?" Alice said.

"There's still a lot humans don't know about the supernatural. Hell, there's a lot of things we don't know about each other," Harriet said. It always surprised her how fragmented the supernatural community was. Werewolves were very close knit, and so were witches, both being centred around family and community, but they never interacted with the other group. And vampires and demons theoretically should get on, as both were immortal beings that ran in social circles since they couldn't reproduce naturally.

"But the labs were opened after the reveal when people were scared. What questions could they possibly want to know that they can't just ask a supernatural?" Alice asked.

Harriet didn't want to think about it because whatever answers they were looking for, they were looking for them in one of her friends.

"What if they're using them for something? You said no vampires or werewolves were taken. What if the government is training them, magical warfare?" Alice said. She was sat in the backseat with Petal. Dan hadn't wanted to bring the dog without any way of strapping her in, but Alice insisted she'd be fine.

"Magical warfare? I think that's a bit too conspiracy theory," Dan said. He'd mostly remained quiet throughout their stakeout so far.

Alice's face deadpanned. "We're literally sat outside a facility with armed guards in a small Welsh village. How much more conspiracy would you like?"

"I'd insist on a dark and stormy night," Dan bit back, clearly not in the mood for sarcasm.

Harriet wouldn't admit it a loud in front of Dan, for fear of getting her head metaphorically bitten off, but she thought Alice had a point. Maybe not for magic warfare, but certainly to research magic, witches and demons were revealed almost as the initial labs were shutting down, and very few were taken into them. Ms Pickett seemed to be a rare case of a witch being there longer than a few weeks. Considering also that witches hoarded their knowledge, even from other covens, it was difficult to know even what the extent of a witch's magic was.

After the reveal of witches, many had cried out for the labs to stay open, and almost won on a near vote. Humans were uncomfortable with the idea of people walking among them, with no visible markers, who could kill them with a thought or turn the whole world purple without a second thought. Witches had argued no one had the power or the inclination to do either of those things, but they did have a council who monitored illegal magic and persecuted those who crossed their rules.

The council operated even more secretly than most witches did. The most anyone had been able to tell was that any necromancy, love spells, or murdering was illegal, but mostly that whatever was illegal for humans was also illegal for witches. They also knew that despite what fortune tellers had said, any type of time travel or prophecy was impossible, this had mostly been raised over concerns about the lottery, rather than them using it to hurt anybody.

"How are we going to get in?" Alice asked, after tactfully not rising to Dan's sarcasm.

It was the question that had been floating around the car, waiting for someone to say it since they rolled up and found the entire facility lit up and fully running. They were currently parked off the main road, tucked behind the corner of a small building, most likely the old gardener's shed. Harriet was at least more sure that what they were looking at was an old college. It was too small to be a university.

"Well, we're not, are we? We'd never get past the guards at the front gate. Who knows what security they have inside," Dan said, looking quite like he'd like to put his foot down and drive straight through the gate and in through the front doors.

"And what would we even do when we're in there?" Harriet said, wishing Dan would put his foot down, and they could run in and grab Connor from there.

"We need proof!" Alice said insistently.

Harriet and Dan both simultaneously made questioning noises and turned slightly to look at Alice. She was perched on the edge of the seat and looked hopeful.

"The police already knew about this place, right? But they haven't gone in yet, so clearly they don't have any evidence that any wrong doing is going on in there, otherwise they'd have a warrant, right?"

"Yeah?" Harriet asked.

"So," Alice paused, as if Harriet and Dan were supposed to instantly get it, "So we get kidnapped, get a video camera or something and film it, then the police would have proof and could shut the place down."

"There are so many things wrong with that," Dan started angrily. Harriet tried to shush him, but he full turned in his seat and let loose. "No, that's a terrible idea, that's the idea that got Connor kidnapped in the first place. The last thing we want to do is get someone else kidnapped. Also, then what? You've got your footage but how are you going to get out then? You can't, you'd have your footage, but you'd be stuck in there like everyone else."

Alice's face had gone stony. Harriet could see that her eyes had welled up, "I'm just trying to put suggestions out there, better than some," she snapped back. "Glaring at the door isn't going to get him out."

"And neither is throwing another witch on the bonfire," Dan said, turning back sharply to face the front.

Alice and Harriet sucked in a breath.

"Dan," Harriet warned.

"No, she's being stupid and we both know it. Witches," he scoffed, in a full rage, "think they're so much smarter than everyone else. It's her fault that Connor's in there, and now she's trying to feed us the same rubbish."

"You think I don't know that Connor is there because of me?" Alice rasped. Harriet could see the tears teetering on the edge, waiting to run down her face.

Silence filled the car, as Dan refused to answer her. Harriet wanted to break the tension but wasn't sure it was possible or that anything would be even vaguely appropriate at this stage.

She couldn't help but feel they were never going to get Connor out at this rate. They'd failed to find out what was happening with Mr Jones in time, and he'd been kidnapped. Even if he were a bad guy, they'd still failed, and now she was terrified they were going to fail Connor now, when it mattered. She kept remembering some of the things that had been done to her in the labs, relentless experiments to test everything from the thickness of her skin to the demented dentist visits, strapped to the chair like something from a horror movie.

Harriet had been all for using animals for scientific advancement until she'd become a lab rat herself. Since the labs, she'd never taken another science degree for fear she'd end up crying over a dissected rat.

After the labs, humans had breathed a sigh of relief that they better understood the monsters that walked among them, and therefore they could no longer hurt them. Supernatural lived in constant fear the monsters would start experimenting again.

"Right," Harriet said, having had enough of the silence in the car, and enough of staring at the building, wondering which room Connor was in, whether he was wondering where the hell they all were. "We're no use out here arguing. Let's go home and come back with an idea of how to get in. All of us, meet in the library tomorrow. I'll get Simon to find out as much about the building's history as possible and who owns it now."

Dan stayed silent but quietly started the car and started driving them home.

*

He dropped Alice off first. He didn't switch the car off and help her like he had previously done. Harriet got the feeling she reminded him a lot of his sister. Although Harriet had to feel for Dan's mum, sibling fights must be vicious if all the siblings were werewolves. Hormones did not mix well with lycanthropy. Harriet couldn't imagine what state the house must be in. Werewolf fights tended to always end physically.

Harriet helped Alice and Petal out of the car. Apart from her red rimmed eyes, you wouldn't have been able to tell anything was wrong.

"Stay safe," Harriet said, before getting back in the car. Dan at least waited until Alice was safely in the house with the door locked behind her, before speeding off.

Harriet lingered halfway out the car when Dan dropped her off at her own flat. She wasn't quite sure what she wanted to say to him; whether to yell at him for making Alice cry or wanted to worry at him about what was possibly happening to Connor right now.

"We'll find a way in," she promised. "Even if it kills me."

He looked at her. "The things my mum said about what went on in there. I can't stop thinking about—" He paused and took a deep breath. "We have to get in soon."

Harriet nodded. "Alice was right you know. The easiest way in is going to be to get kidnapped ourselves."

"They won't take *us*," he said. "They only take demons and witches. Besides, even if they didn't already know our faces, they certainly already know Alice's. They'd never take her. Too much of a risk with us snooping around."

"They took Connor," Harriet said, although she understood where he was coming from.

"I was thinking about that. I think maybe he asked too many questions; they panicked and took him. I don't see them doing it for his magic. He has so little compared to any other witch, it wouldn't make sense if they're using their magic, or even testing it," he added before Harriet argued.

"They still might take Alice, if she asked too many questions as well," Harriet said, although even she was doubting it. They didn't have any leverage, so they'd probably just ignore Alice, save raising any more red flags.

"How would she get back out again? How would she even sneak around the place and find Connor? She's blind!" Dan said.

Harriet rolled her eyes. "She's managed just fine for the last 16 years."

"I don't think 'fine' covers breaking into a top-secret research facility and breaking out one of its prisoners," Dan snarked.

"Fine. So, if they're not going to kidnap us, and Alice can't go, who are they going to kidnap?" Harriet asked.

They both sat there in silence, debating how many witches they knew who would be up for getting kidnapped and illegally breaking and entering.

Suddenly, there was a loud bang emitted from Harriet's building, and Dan arm flew out in front of her instinctively. Harriet was about to make a soccer mom joke when it hit her.

"Oh my god. I know how we're getting in. I'll see you tomorrow," she said, hoping out of the car. Dan looked sceptical about her entering her building, "I need to have a chat with the flat upstairs!"

Chapter Sixteen

Harriet finally finished talking with the coven at 8 am, which, unfortunately for her, had carried on far too early into the morning, and she wouldn't be able to get back through the corridors to get down to the basement with comfy concrete walls because she'd have to pass all the windows on her way to the stairs.

She was resigning herself to ask the coven whether she could sleep under someone's desk, or any place out of sight from a window, when one of the lads dragged a heavyweight blanket out for her, possibly a fire blanket by the look of it, although she suspected any blanket that lived in this flat for longer than a week ended up with scorch marks on it.

They dragged it over her, and she ended up bowing slightly under the weight of it. Harriet tucked it up around her face so only her eyes peaked out.

"There you are," Jack said triumphantly.

Harriet made her way down the corridor slowly, mostly due to the weight of the blanket. Every time she came across a window, she would hike the blanket over her face and run past the light source. She felt like an excited child whose parents had thrown a bed sheet over them for Halloween and called it a day.

An excited child, nonetheless, who had just worked out how to break into a top-secret government facility.

*

The library was quiet when Harriet entered the following evening. She had messaged everyone to meet her there as soon after sunset as possible. She had felt slightly bad dragging everyone out of bed constantly, and having them all revolve around her sleep schedule, but there was little alternative unless she wore multiple layers and carried an umbrella inside. At least this way they also got Simon's help. Harriet had messaged Cora, but she had said she couldn't make it away for that long, but she'd do some digging in the background, whatever she could find on the building and help them however she could with their plan.

Harriet sat in the library at a large table at the back. She waved to Simon, and he told her she was the first one here so far, but he'd join them when everyone had arrived.

She knew that Dan's pack had practically pushed him to take time off, as he'd previously worked the evening shift every day, and had done since they opened, barring pack events and such, but the coffee shop was closed then anyway as it was only the pack who worked there. So, she felt less guilty about dragging him out at all hours.

She had felt bad for Alice, as Harriet knew she was either in school during the day, or ran the magic shop on weekends, and so keeping her up all night wasn't helping. Alice had insisted she attended today's meeting despite Harriet saying it was fine if she needed to sleep. Alice said she wasn't going to be able to sleep anyway, so she may as well be helpful.

Harriet had wondered if there was anything that she could do to help. She noticed that the witches above her seemed to be up all hours whenever she went to see them. She wondered if they had a spell or potion that kept them awake or if they did shifts. As there always seemed to be something bubbling in the cauldron when she went, previous potions crusted onto the side like any well-used cookware.

"Hey." Dan sat down in front of her, and Harriet jumped.

"Jesus, you scared the life out of me!" she said.

"Sorry, so what's this plan to get into the facility?" he asked, not sounding sorry at all.

"I'll tell you when everyone else gets here," Harriet said, looking behind her, as if everyone was suddenly going to come walking through the door.

"Harriet," Dan said, his eyebrows furrowing in annoyance.

Harriet sighed, and gave once last glance towards the door. Alice may have fallen asleep, as she was not normally one to be late. The coven always struck Harriet as the type to be running at least half an hour behind the rest of the world. She had no evidence, but it was a gut feeling.

"Fine," she said. "There's a coven that live above me of three male witches." Dan's eyebrows looked suitably impressed, so she continued, "I am hoping it will make the prospect of kidnapping them more enticing. If the facility is experimenting on witches, the chance to see why the number of male witches has increased must surely be on the list, and so far, all the kidnapped victims are female."

"Apart from Connor," Dan said.

Harriet nodded, "But we don't actually know how magic Connor is. He's not a proper, full-fledged and trained witch."

Dan made a noise that Harriet interpreted to mean, 'I suppose that's true', but he didn't sound convinced.

"So, the coven are getting kidnapped," Dan said. "But how are we getting in? And more importantly, out?"

"So, I'm not sure of the exact way, they said they'd have a think and come up with something by today, and then if everyone agrees we were thinking about going tonight."

"Tonight?" Dan's eyebrows shot up.

Harriet nodded, "I know it's short notice, but I don't want to leave Connor in there too long, it's only been two days but even two days in one of those labs is enough to scar you."

Dan's expression hardened. He nodded. "Okay, I'll text my pack, to let them know where I'm going. I—I have a responsibility to look after them so I can't just go missing for days on end. We need a guarantee we can get back out of the facility."

"Okay."

They waited for another 10 minutes and Alice showed up, and promptly dozed off in her seat as soon as she sat down. The bags under her eyes were purple and her face was clean from its normal heavy makeup, making her look years younger. The coven arrived about half an hour after they were meant to and Harriet felt weirdly proud for being correct.

They looked scruffy, despite trying to dress up a bit, on the chance of needing to blend in at the club later. Two of them even had dirt smudged on their cheeks. Simon looked horrified when they walked in and looked as if he was tempted to send them back out until they cleaned up. Simon, of course, was wearing his usual button up and sweater vest, and was not coming to the club later.

Once everyone had sat around the table, looking like the oddest study group possible, Harriet laid out what she had already told Dan, and then let the coven pick it up from there.

"So basically," Jack said, as he seemed to be the ringleader of the group. "We were thinking it's more likely they're gonna wanna kidnap us if it's just the one right, that's the MO so far, picking up witches one at a time. So basically, I'm gonna get kidnapped, and we're gonna shrink everyone else so you can fit on my person, and then you get kidnapped with me, because they bag check and stuff at the so—" Jack got cut off when Alice interrupted.

"But shrinking spells are illegal," she said, mostly instinctually it seemed as she didn't seem shocked when Jack replied that breaking into government facilities is also illegal. She only made a small comment that they didn't know it was a government facility, it could be privately owned.

"Either way, the bar is gonna check bags at the door, so we're gonna shrink everyone until they fit in one of these." Jack held up a small pouch with a long string attached. "It's normally used by witches to put protective herbs and stuff in, so it won't look out of place, and then I'll just put it around my neck." He demonstrated. The bag was no bigger than the palm of Harriet hand. She wasn't sure how shrinking spells worked, but they were going to need to be tiny.

"The spell will wear off in about three hours or so, so if we get to that point and I still haven't been kidnapped. then we'll have to go to the bathroom and redo the spell."

Alice scoffed. "You want to use it twice back to back?"

"Why?" Dan said suspiciously, looking from the coven to Alice. "Does it have side effects?"

"No," the coven said; at the same time Alice said, "Yes."

"Well, technically," Jack said, "But we've done it three times in a row before and it's not affected us any," he defended.

"Well," Hayden said. "I'm sure I used to be two inches taller."

Jack rolled his eyes, "You're a hypochondriac." Harriet wasn't sure if he was joking or not. She would be surprised if a hypochondriac did half the things that coven tried.

"So, you're going to shrink us, get kidnapped and we'll what? Grow back in the car on the way over and suddenly there's six people instead of one?"

Jack shook his head, "If we get the timings right, we should be able to get kidnapped, and when we arrive at the facility, I'll dispose of the pouch somewhere on route, and so when you guys grow back, you should be in the facility with no staff around, hopefully. We did the best we could with limited information."

Harriet supposed she couldn't ask for much more. She was already asking they get kidnapped and taken into a lab where they may be experimented on before they could get them back out.

"Okay, thank you," she added emphatically, so they knew how much she appreciated them doing this.

"Why are you helping us?" Dan asked, glaring suspiciously at the coven. "There's no upside for you. You get taken into this lab, we can't guarantee any of us will come back out. Why on earth would you agree to this?"

The coven stayed silent for a second before Liam said quietly, "We all grew up not far from each other. My coven took in Jack when his abandoned him."

"Traditionalist," Jack interjected. "Couldn't have a boy in the family line."

"Heartless traditionalists," Liam agreed. "And Hayden lived in the next town. Our covens thought it was important for us to socialise with other boys, so we didn't think we were weird, or—"

"Abnormal," Jack said bitterly.

"Yeah, so we all grew up together, and most covens near us wouldn't give us the time of day. Even our own covens didn't teach us as much as they taught the girls, our education wasn't as important. There was one witch from the Davies coven that taught us though. She would let us read some of the books and she would give us biscuits and stuff while we were there, teach us anything we didn't understand."

They were all grinning fondly. "Isadora, she must have been what, mid-twenties, thirties, said she couldn't have kids, so she had no one to teach, so she'd have to teach us," Liam said.

"She always pretended to be put out, but we knew she enjoyed it, and she didn't even treat us weirdly because we were boys," Jack said.

"And then, we don't know, we think her coven found out she was teaching us, and they sold her out to the labs, because witches were barely even known about back then, but she was taken."

"When she came back," Jack continued, "She—we heard about some of the stuff that happened in those things. I mean we were all only like 10 at the time so a lot of what we heard was filtered, but she wasn't the same when she came back. She was sharp and mean. We went round to see her not long after she got back and she screamed at us to leave her alone, that she didn't want to see us again."

All three of them looked heartbroken, "We don't know exactly what she went through in there, but we didn't want it happening to your friend."

Alice gasped quietly. "The Davies coven? Her name was Isadora Pickett, wasn't it?"

They nodded and Harriet's jaw dropped. Bloody small Welsh towns.

*

The coven had not taken well to the fact that Pickett was in danger of being taken back into these labs again, and they only became more determined to take the facility down.

Harriet had been planning to remind everyone of the risks, and that no one should feel obligated to come with them, and it didn't mean they wouldn't want to get Connor back as much as anyone else. She thought the coven were going to take far more persuading than they actually did. They had been surprisingly motivated to come, solely based on the idea that they would get to break into a research facility. Now they had found out they had a chance to help Pickett out, they seemed impatient to get started.

"You have no idea how much it meant to all of us when she helped us when even our own families weren't putting that much faith into us," Jack had said to Harriet quietly when everyone was getting ready to leave. She'd asked him why they wanted to help a woman they hadn't seen in 20 years who'd screamed at them the last time she'd seen them.

Harriet supposed she could understand that. It was just she was having trouble reconciling the sweet-sounding Isadora with the cold Ms Pickett.

"Her coven was uber traditionalist, more so than the one I was born into," Jack said when Harriet explained her hesitation. "We did some digging when we were older. Her coven almost kicked her out for not being able to have kids." Harriet's face must have conveyed her shock as Jack made an 'I know, right?' noise. "It's all about continuing the family line, but they let her stay but made her know she should be thankful for it, and then they found her tutoring the local boy witches, and that was it. When she came out of the labs, the coven took her back, figured it had scared her into sorting out her behaviour." Jack looked disgusted, "It must have done if you say she's as traditionalist as she is now."

"This is all a very touching backstory, but don't you think we should be heading to the club?" Dan said impatiently, having already gathered all his things

115

and was standing waiting to leave. Alice, Hayden, and Liam were all stood next to him, although none of them looked as angry as Dan.

Harriet gave Dan a swift kick as she passed him to let him know he was being a jackass. He seemed to get the message, as he didn't say anything else.

"Right," Harriet said grimly. "Let's go break into a government facility."

Jack grinned, "Where's your enthusiasm?"

"Don't go mad and be safe," Simon lectured her as they started heading for the doors en masse.

"Are you sure you don't want to come?" Harriet asked, already knowing he wasn't going to.

"Someone has to stay behind in case none of you come back." He said it lightly, but Harriet could see the genuine worry in his eyes. Harriet and Simon had had a separate conversation about her going back into these labs, and what to do if she didn't come back out, and Simon had the names of the police officers they'd spoken to.

"Be safe," he said. Harriet nodded, because she couldn't promise that she would.

"What? Come with us," Liam said loudly, already most of the way to the door, as Simon and Harriet had hung back.

Simon gave a flat look. "I'm too old to be breaking into government buildings." Despite looking as young as the day he was bitten at 24.

"What? Come on, you're never too old to get in trouble." Liam said cheekily, although he wasn't genuinely pushing now. Harriet joined everyone else at the door.

"I'm a 317," Simon called back.

Harriet laughed and pushed a gawking Liam through the door.

Chapter Seventeen

They parked around the corner from the club and got ready for Jack to do the shrinking spell on the pavement by the car. They got some odd looks from people passing by, most of whom were in clubbing gear. The six of them were stood in a loose circle all looking like they were going to different events; the coven were dressed like rumpled uni students, Dan was conspicuously wearing all black, Alice was wearing a school uniform, and Harriet had her standard 'going out in sunlight' outfit on consisting of several layers, gloves, hat, and an unopened umbrella. Petal was wearing a neckerchief, and looked to be the smartest dressed one there.

She didn't know what was going to happen at the lab, and she didn't know how long they were going to be in there for, so she figured she was better safe than sorry, and had worn almost every article of clothing she owned.

"Right," Jack said. "Everybody ready?"

"Does it hurt?" Alice asked. "I've never been shrunk before,"

Liam shook his head, "Not really, you just get that jolting feeling like you've been dropped down an elevator shaft."

"Great," Alice said dryly, although she looked slightly more reassured.

"Okay, Liam and Hayden are gonna shrink you guys and then I'll shrink them, so no one is too worn out," Jack said, as Liam moved towards Alice and Harriet, and Hayden grudgingly stepped closer to Dan.

Harriet noticed Alice shifting slightly, and figured she was probably still slightly on edge about being on the other end of magic she'd never done herself. It must be unnerving, knowing fully what could be done and having to place blind trust in the lads you only knew from occasionally coming to your shop.

"I'll go first," Harriet volunteered to Liam.

"Okay," he said, and then placed his hands on Harriet's shoulders before muttering some words to himself. Harriet suddenly felt a tingling sensation sweep through her body before she felt the dropping feeling Liam mentioned as she plummeted down to being centimetres tall.

"This is so weird," Harriet said, looking at the giant pair of boots in front of her. She craned her neck up but she could only just make out Liam's face, like the top of a skyscraper.

"Bloody hell," Dan's voice said. Harriet could only just hear him, she turned to see him, and he looked as though he were several streets away in distance, when he'd only been a few steps away previously. She supposed it was all relative.

He jogged over to her, and they both went and met Alice, who was a shorter distance away, and she and Petal were now a similar size to themselves.

"Am I small?" Alice asked. "I felt the dropping feeling, but I don't feel any different," she said, patting herself drown as if she could feel the change in height somehow.

"Yeah, we all are," Harriet said. She could see Liam and Hayden making their way over.

"Okay," Liam said. "Jack is going to grab the pouch for us all to get into. Fair warning, it's going to be bumpy." He grinned. "I hope no one gets travel sickness," he said, looking concerned about their wellbeing or the fact the thought hadn't occurred to him before. Harriet wasn't sure which.

They all shook their heads.

"Good." Liam breathed a sigh of relief.

Jack, who now looked like a giant from a fairy-tale, placed the pouch down on the ground next to them. It looked less like a pouch now and more like a giant cave. Hayden clambered into it first, and then held his hand out to help them rest of the up.

Harriet noticed that Jack had bent to tie his shoelaces, as to not draw attention to the five shrunken friends that were in front of him, no doubt. Harriet hoped the coven had made sure no one was looking when they cast the spell because Harriet had forgotten to check.

Alice and Petal were in the pouch, Harriet and Hayden followed, then Dan and Liam brought up the rear.

Harriet heard the booming whisper of 'Sorry' from Jack, and barely had time to wonder what he was apologising for before the pouch tilted slowly into the upright position and its content, namely them, all tumbled to the bottom of the bag. They gave up trying to rearrange themselves until the bag raised up and over Jack's head, before settling down around his neck.

There was enough room in the pouch for them all to sit in two lines facing each other; Harriet, Alice and Petal on one side, facing Dan, Liam and Hayden. Their crossed legs were knocking against each other, but they all had room to lean back against the fabric, which acted as a sort of recliner.

Liam and Hayden had switched the torches on the phones on and had placed them screen down on the floor to give some light into the bag. Harriet could see Jack had left the top of the pouch open for air, but given the fact it was night-time, there wasn't any light coming through it.

They sat in silence for a short while. Eventually, Jack must have reached the front of the line as they heard the bouncer at the door, and Jack's reply, "Jack Fletcher, Fletcher coven."

"So, it's Jack's coven?" Harriet asked.

"Yeah," Liam said. "Me and Jack got kicked out of my coven, and Hayden out of his, improper behaviour." He smirked. "Jack's the oldest out of us so when we formed our own it was his coven, but just in name, because there's only three of us, all decisions get made between us, we didn't want all that coven formality stuff."

"Normally," Alice said in Harriet and Dan's direction, "When a coven member breaks off to start a family even if they change their name, they still have their coven name. So, Pickett would have been her married name, but she was still in the Davies coven."

"Yeah, I think they wanted her to change it back to Davies after they found out she couldn't have kids," Liam said sadly.

Alice nodded, "I image so. They definitely tried to make her change it after she and her husband separated. He left after she got taken to the labs. Apparently, that's how he found out she was a witch. There was a lot of gossip, apparently. I asked my mum after Connor asked if I could find out anything about Pickett."

"How old are you guys, then?" Dan asked Liam and Hayden, "You said you were about 10 when the labs were open. I thought you were younger."

"I'm 27," Liam said.

"He's the baby," Hayden teased. "I'm 28 and Jack is 30."

Dan's eyebrows shot up. "You don't look it." Although it had the undertone of 'You don't act it'.

"It's our youthful outlook on life," Hayden deadpanned, and Liam snorted.

Dan rolled his eyes, but didn't argue, they all lulled into silence.

The noises from outside the bag were indiscernible from each other, which meant they had no idea how well the plan was going.

"How do we know when he's been kidnapped?" Alice asked, clearly thinking along the same lines as Harriet was.

"When we get let out, I suppose," Liam said. Which wasn't really reassuring.

"So why are shrinking spells illegal?" Harriet asked. They had time to kill while they waited for Jack to get kidnapped. "I know love spells and resurrection and that are illegal but why shrinking spells?"

"It depends on the context," Alice said, "Shrinking objects is fine. Like, if you shrink your clothes to fit in your suitcase better, shrinking objects lasts for hours. Shrinking humans is more complex, hence shorter shrinking times, but they're illegal because what use is airport security if you can shrink someone to fit in your luggage?"

Harriet thought about it for a minute, but apparently Dan had gotten interested now as well. "But what about drugs? You could shrink them small enough security probably wouldn't find them. What about that?"

"Drugs are still illegal for witches as well," Hayden smirked. "But human shoved drugs up their bums and all sorts, if you're trying to do something illegally, most will find a way, magic or not. The magic council is there to make sure we don't have too much of an unfair advantage."

"So, what do the magic council do, then? Can they sense when someone does a spell like this?" Harriet asked.

"No," Liam said, much nicer to her than Hayden was to Dan, although she supposed she hadn't shouted at Jack earlier. "They act like the police do, like a special division, and if the police have cases that have magical crimes, they'll hand it off to them."

"And what are the punishments? Banishment or can you have your magic taken off of you?"

Liam shook his head. "You can't strip someone's magic, and if you banish them, they could still do magic. No, they have these special suppression jails set up, so your magic can't penetrate the walls. You can't take someone's magic off them or stop it, but you can confine it to one room so they can't escape or hurt someone."

"Oh, yeah, no, I've heard about those." It was one of the only things they had time to test on the witches in labs. They'd had limited time, so the first thing humans wanted to know was how to suppress someone's magic, to make them less of a threat, all done for personal security. Harriet knew about magic jails; she'd just thought something as impressive sounding as the magic council would do something more than your average judge does.

The conversation was derailed when they suddenly all went flying, as the bag went sailing in the air, as if Jack had spun around very quickly.

"That bugger better not be dancing!" Hayden grumbled, as they all righted themselves.

The bag stopped moving as Jack did. "I don't think he is," Harriet said. It was impossible to tell what was going on outside the bag, though.

Suddenly, they all felt the heavy vibration as Jack let out a hearty laugh.

"It's safe to assume he's not in danger then," Harriet said.

"That bugger better not be chatting up some girl," Hayden said.

"He wouldn't," Liam assured Harriet and Dan. "Not in this situation, not when he's here for business." Hayden seemed to agree with Liam, so Harriet figured it was the truth.

"So, I know some stuff is illegal but is there anything that magic can't do? Like are there limitations on it?" Harriet asked, getting back to their previous conversation when they realised that they probably wouldn't be able to figure out anything else that was going on.

"You can't create matter. You can alter what's there, but you can't magic anything into existence," Alice said.

"So, you can duplicate food, but not create it?" Dan asked, Alice nodded. "So why is world hunger still a thing, if witches can magic extra food?"

Harriet was sure he didn't mean it to come out quite as accusing as it did, but Harriet kind of wanted to know as well. It was a fair question.

Alice seemed to take it as Dan (hopefully) meant it, rather than how he said it. "You can duplicate supplies going out, and some witches have been doing it in secret for years, but we can't do it on a large scale because the government is scared if they give witches a good name and too much power, they'll take over or something ridiculous."

"So, they're shooting themselves in the foot," Harriet said.

"Don't humans always?" Alice grinned. There were several huffs of laughter from around the bag, when Harriet suddenly realised how quiet it had gone outside of the bag.

"Guys, I can't hear anything," Harriet said, and everyone simultaneously raised one of their ears towards the top of the bag, as if that would help them hear anything.

The background noise quietened even more as Jack was possibly led into a private room. Harriet could make out two distinguished, albeit muffled, voices. One was clearly Jack's, mostly going from the fact they could feel the vibrations of him talking given the fact they were rested on his chest. The other was quieter from being further away, but was definable by its accent, that if Harriet was pressed to make a guess, sounded vaguely like it could be a Scottish accent.

"I think this is the Scottish man. The barman said he heard Connor talking to a Scottish man before he disappeared," Harriet said, and everyone sat up straighter.

Harriet wasn't sure exactly how long the conversation lasted, but she would guess at least 10 or 15 minutes. The voices went back and forth, before they jolted upwards and started moving.

"It doesn't seem like he'd being dragged anywhere," Liam whispered, although no one outside of the bag was going to hear them anyway. The motion of the bag seemed exactly as it had when Jack was walking into the club. They all jumped when a door slammed loudly. A fire exit, possibly.

"Are we heading out the back of the building?" Harriet asked.

Another voice spoke, one that wasn't Jack or Scottish sounding. Harriet still couldn't make out what was being said.

Jack, and subsequently the bag, jolted downwards, and a car door slammed. Another door opened and shut from somewhere in front of them, and then the engine revved and the car pulled off.

"Do you reckon we just got kidnapped?" Harriet asked hopefully.

Chapter Eighteen

The car journey took a long time; long enough that Harriet was worried the spell was going to wear off before they got there. They'd spent over an hour in the club, and they seemed close to an hour in the car now.

Dan seemed to be sharing her thoughts. "If the facility is on the Hampstead Estate, then it should have taken us 15 minutes to get there going direct. Unless they're driving in circles a bit, so it makes it harder for the person the find it,"

Harriet hadn't considered that. "That's probably it."

Liam looked doubtful. "It's been an hour and a half." He showed his watch as if they didn't believe him. Harriet hadn't realised it had been that long. "Besides if we were still in town we would have turned once in a while, we've been going straight for 10 minutes. I think we're on the motorway."

"Why would we be on the motorway? Where else would they take us?" Harriet asked. Maybe they had a second location, although she doubted it.

"What if they worked out what we were doing?" Dan said.

Harriet shook her head. "They didn't know Jack's face, let alone that he knew us. Why would they be suspicious?"

Liam joined in, "Jack's really subtle as well. No way he gave himself away."

"I still don't like it," Dan said.

"None of us do," Harriet said, and they all settled uneasily into the silence and the rocking of the journey.

They finally arrived at their destination and the clock was ticking closer to the spell wearing off. The spell reversing wasn't a set time, more of a general estimate, making it difficult to time correctly, which had everyone shuffling with nerves.

Jack finally got out of the car and seemed to be led in somewhere. There was the whoosh of automatic doors, and echoing footsteps across polished floors in large empty rooms.

They heard an elevator ding, and then after a minute the quiet 'Floor Twelve' by the automated voice.

Jack was led to a room. The man who was leading him said, "*Through here.*"

"*So, what now?*" they heard Jack ask. "*I thought we were going to the facility. This looks like an office block.*"

There was an unkind laugh that followed, "*Boss heard what you and your friends were up to, asked to bring you to HQ instead. Tell your friends to come out of hiding wherever they are. Boss'll be here in a minute.*"

A door slammed shut.

Harriet swore.

*

The top of the drawstring pouch opened, and they saw Jack's eye peering in. "They're onto us. I don't think they know how I've smuggled you in, but they know you're here or they're bluffing. Maybe we should pretend I came on my own."

"Too late," Liam called, before the spell wore off and they collectively tore through the pouch and landed on Jack in what looked like a scrimmage.

Once the five of them and the dog managed to arrange themselves off of Jack and sat on the floor next to him, he was rubbing his ribs. "I think you've cracked my ribs, except you Petal, you did nothing wrong," he said with levity, but also underlaid with a genuine wince.

Liam put his fingers lightly across Jack ribs, and Harriet saw a light that was more like a glow briefly surround Liam's fingers before dying down. Jack stretched out his torso afterwards.

"It was barely bruised, you big baby," Liam rolled his eyes.

"Well, that's gonna come in handy," Dan said bluntly.

"Oh, I don't—I'm not medically trained. I can't do much more than healing ribs and such, and that's only because I had so much practice when we were little," Liam said.

Harriet remembered Alice saying that she'd only get someone who was a doctor as well as a witch to magically operate on her eyes. "So you can't perform magic outside of your own basis of knowledge?"

"Exactly," Liam said, "I know how bruises heal and can repair capillaries, but I don't know how to reset broken bones or remove bullets without causing damage or anything like that."

"Any witch can take away pain to the extent that paracetamol could. Providing you know how it works, you can manipulate your magic to work the same, but someone in pharmacology could act like a morphine drip if they practiced the magic," Alice joined in. "It's why covens specialise, and no two magic users will have the same arsenal of spells. Witches are far more like humans than we ever admit."

"So, don't go getting yourself shot," Hayden said to Dan, "Because none of us know how to remove the bullet without causing organ damage."

Dan rolled his eyes, "Well I'm glad this has been a learning experience for all involved but that doesn't explain what we're going to do about the situation we're in."

Jack nodded. "Right, well, I wouldn't advise shrinking again this close to the last time, not if it can be avoided, as it's technically not a regulated spell yet—"

"What?" Alice said.

"—And so, the side effects are not as widely tested as advised, and they already know we're here, anyway," Jack finished.

"Damn it," Harriet said. She looked towards the door. The boss still hadn't come through but as she looked around, she realised they were in somebody's office. It was large and polished and could very well be the boss'.

"What did they say to you?" Harriet asked Jack. "When they kidnapped you from the bar, you were talking to the Scottish man, weren't you?" Harriet got up and started looking around the room. Everything was put away, nothing left out to take a glance at, she tried the drawers on the desk and they were locked.

"Um, yeah. I mean, it was a bit weird, he was talking like it was a damn job interview, although if they knew it was me trying to get kidnapped, he wouldn't have had to exactly put a bag over my head and shove me in the car, would he?" Jack said, he and the coven started looking around as well. Dan started towards the door, but Jack waved him off. "He locked it when he left."

Harriet winced. She hadn't even thought to try the door. She wondered what that said about her mentality if she went straight for the locked drawers rather than the means of escape. She was pretty sure she'd taken a psychology course once that told her, although she'd taken it back when Freud was the big thing and she certainly hoped they'd moved on since then.

Suddenly, the lock clicked in the door, and it swung open. A woman walked in with her head downcast towards her phone, typing away.

She seemed to realise that there were other people in the room and she did a double take as she looked up. "What the hell are you guys doing here?"

"Cora?" Harriet asked in disbelief.

Chapter Nineteen

"Cora, what the hell are you doing here?" Harriet said.

"I work here. What are you doing here and who are these guys?" she asked, gesturing to the coven.

"These are the guys I said were helping me get into the facility. They're witches," Harriet said.

"They haven't done a very good job. This is an office block," Cora huffed, "The facility is on the Hampstead Estate in town. I was digging into it like you asked and I think my boss is involved."

"No duh," Jack said, "I got kidnapped and told I was about to meet him."

Cora looked confused. "He left like an hour ago. He's basically never here. I have to do all the bloody paperwork." She sighed and dropped a folder on the desk that had been previously tucked neatly under her arm. "So, he is connected." She sighed. She sat on the edge of the desk in a slumped position.

"What's wrong?" Harriet asked.

"I finally found a position that worked, supernatural friendly, decent pay. Yeah sure, I had to be his bloody secretary, but I basically did the job for him. I figured someone would take note and I'd actually be given a proper position at some point." Cora put her face in her hands, "And it turns out he's kidnapping young girls. Ugh, I could kill him."

"Surely, there's been signs. I mean, you said you basically run his life. it can't be a massive surprise," Hayden said. Cora glared at him.

Harriet didn't feel like she knew Hayden well enough to kick him like she would have it if had been Dan saying it. Jack kicked Hayden on her behalf.

"Like I said," Cora frowned. "He's barely ever here. I assumed he had another business. A couple of the higher ups run a couple of side businesses." She scoffed. "Can't trust that bloody Welsh accent, makes them sound so sweet and unassuming."

Harriet and Dan looked at each other over Cora bent head:

"*Mr Jones*?" Dan mouthed.

Harriet frowned, and morosely mouthed, "*Could be*," back at him.

"What's his name?" Dan asked.

"Well, he always introduced himself as Ian Pritchard, but there was some documentation for a Joe Mans and passport for Kevin Williams, so I have no idea which was his real name, if any of them were," Cora said. "Obviously, it rang a few alarm bells. No one has a spare identity for rainy days unless they're involved in dodgy stuff. At first, I thought maybe he was importing illegal strength vodka or something low level and was being precautious, and I remembered about your bar and how they were importing illegally, so I started digging. That was a couple of weeks ago…"

Cora trailed off hesitantly, and Harriet was immediately on red alert. "What did you find?"

Cora winced "I may have found that the bar had particular payments being made to it from Ian or whatever his name was, and I looked into it further and found that Ian also has a building registered in Joe Mans' name, which is the building in Hampstead, which has a roster of employees who are mostly either military or scientists."

"Why didn't you tell us?" Harriet and Dan demanded.

"Because," Cora hissed, glancing at the door as if someone would come running in if they heard shouting, which was actually a high possibility, "we used to have adventures at uni, right? We actually helped that girl find her missing brother once, do you remember? Or when we found out the teachers had that gambling pool going, and the sports teacher was actually dabbling in illegal dog fighting and we got him arrested? Or when we accidentally set fire to a lecture hall and invented a school holiday in the same day?"

"Did you guys actually study at uni at all?" Jack asked.

"What's your point?" Harriet said.

"*They* were adventures," Cora said, "A good laugh and a story to look back on. This though, this is really dangerous. As soon as I found out, I went to the police. I've been giving them information for a while and they are going to be dealing with it. They said it was dangerous for me to be passing on information, let alone you guys investigating it!"

"So, you're their source," Dan said, Harriet gave him a confused look. "When we went to the police, after Connor got kidnapped, the police said they had a source and they were pursuing it. That was you."

Cora nodded.

"Look, I'm sorry I didn't tell you, but you can't investigate," Cora pleaded.

"Sorry, but we're so close to getting Connor back now," Harriet said. "We just need to—"

"No, you can't!" Cora stood, careless of keeping her voice down. "Please, you'll get hurt."

"Connor might already be hurt," Dan argued.

"The police will get him back. You have to sit tight. They'll bring him back and then they'll take down the facility. You just need to give them time!" Cora pleaded. "You're going to be no help to him if you all get stuck in there. No offence, but you've got three untrained male witches, a blind witch, a werewolf who is a barista and yourself," she pointed towards Harriet. "You're not exactly the supernatural A Team." Cora was about as close to crying as vampires could get. Her voice sounded wrecked, as though she was already full on bawling, but the only thing that had happened was that her eyes had gone bloodshot and her cheeks were ruddy. She must have had blood recently.

"Cora, I have been in one of those labs. I don't want Connor in there for as long as he has been, let alone any longer," Harriet said, firm and decided. "You can help us get in, or we will find our own way in."

Harriet felt like Cora's mum a lot, or a long-suffering older sister, particularly when Cora had actually been a teenager, before she'd turned, and she was just a bratty teen who ran away from home often, although Harriet couldn't blame her for that bit. Cora had often fashioned rings of bruises around her wrists and neck, although she was never less than defiant about it when Harriet saw her.

Turning Cora hadn't originally been a part of the plan. Harriet had killed her father, though. Blood had been harder to come by in those days, and therefore more easily justifiable when it had. Harriet was not proud of it, but she probably wouldn't have done it any differently if she had to go back. She had provided an alternative style of living for Cora, and it wasn't long until Cora's defiant nature turned onto wanting to be turned herself.

So, it was a surprise to see Cora looking so scared over Harriet's wellbeing, when she hadn't even looked this scared for her own life when it had been in her father's hands.

"I'm coming too, then," Cora said.

"No," Harriet replied, knowing exactly the outrage that was about to follow.

"But—"

"It'll look suspicious if you disappear and we manage to break into the facility," Jack jumped in. Cora glared at him for his troubles.

"He's right." Dan said. "Plus we don't know the layouts or anything really, so we need someone in contact with the police in case we don't come out." Harriet thought it best not to bring up that Simon was already doing that job.

Cora looked around all of them, et tu Brute style, and finally gave a huff that could only be produced by someone who had spent 200 years being a teenager.

"Fine," she snapped, heading around the desk. "But I don't have any layouts or anything. I hadn't gotten that far. I do know there's a van leaving for the facility in the early hours this morning, so you should be able to get passed security but after that, I don't know how to get you into the building."

She unlocked the drawer with a key she plucked from underneath a lamp and started rummaging through looking for something.

"Mr Jones needs better security," Harriet muttered.

"Your lecturer?" Cora asked. "The one who got shot?"

"Yeah," Harriet said. "We think he might be your boss." She inclined her head towards Dan. "In fact," Harriet said. She had a picture of Mr Jones in his pre-bullet hole body that she'd taken from the university staff page for when they'd initially gone to see Alice, not that it had helped. "Is this him?" Harriet held the picture out towards Cora.

Cora looked up from the drawer she was looking through. "Yeah, it is, He was your lecturer? No wonder he was never here. He did change his appearance not long ago, though, different face, body, everything. I thought he just got bored with his old one."

"It was because he had a rather inconvenient bullet hole in his head," Harriet said, pocketing her phone again. "What are you looking for?" she asked Cora, who had paused in her riffling.

"Hm? Oh, I was trying to find the schedule for the trucks, they go out once a week. I was *told* it was the bins taking all the stuff to recycling and that, but when I started digging I found the company didn't actually exist and it all went downhill from there." She pulled a piece of paper out triumphantly and placed it on the desk.

She flipped through to the third page. "Today." She pointed to it on the page. "4:30AM."

"It does seem like an odd time to take the bins out," Liam said.

Cora nodded, "There are quite a few vampires working here so I didn't think it was too odd at first, but any vampires that were out by the time they reached the nearest tip would have been caught out in sunrise."

"So how do we get in the van?" Jack asked.

"That's the easy part," Cora said. "It's how I smuggle you lot down to the front of the building without anyone seeing in the first place."

Jack grinned madly, "Well if these lot don't mind the potential side effect of losing an inch in height, I know how."

Cora looked confused but Alice gave out a loud and long sigh.

"It does mean you'll end up trying to sneak into the facility during sunlight hours," Cora warned Harriet. "You can still back out?" she added hopefully.

Harriet just grimly waved her umbrella.

Chapter Twenty

Harriet was slightly more apprehensive about been shrunken down now that she knew it was not a registered spell and was something that the coven had cooked up in their spare time.

"Surely there was a registered spell for shrinking humans?" Alice asked.

"Yeah, but you have to apply for spells that could potentially be used for illegal means and so they're not going to let three semi-trained male witches use it, so we had to take the one for shrinking objects and modify it," Jack said, and Alice looked even more horrified than before.

"Come on, you didn't know this earlier, and you were fine, blissful ignorance," Liam grinned, squeezing her shoulder reassuringly.

"We're all going to die," Alice said dramatically.

"That's the spirit," Liam said, with the same mad grin that Jack had.

Cora looked like she was rapidly losing her already shaky confidence in them by the second.

"And what are we getting in this time, because I think we destroyed the bag we were in last time," Dan said, pointing to the remains of the bag on the floor, still by Jack's feet.

"We could use my sock?" Jack suggested.

"There is no way I'm going in your sock," Hayden said. "We'll all be knocked out by the noxious gas before we get to the elevator."

"I'll take you in my pocket," Cora said. "You'll fit, right?" she asked Harriet, Harriet turned in askance to Jack. Jack looked at the pocket Cora was pointing to on her smart suit jacket and nodded.

"Don't see why not. Who's up first?" he asked.

No one volunteered. Harriet sighed and turned to Cora, "You're sure on the timings?"

Cora nodded. "As sure as I can be." They had tried to time it as closely as possible, given that the spell wearing off wasn't going to happen at a set time, so that they would re-grow once they'd had time to get out of the van and make their way inside the building.

"Okay, let's do this," Harriet said, turning towards Jack.

"Isn't there a counter spell that you could do, to grow us again, so we wouldn't have to worry about timings?" Dan asked, before Jack could do anything.

"We hadn't gotten that far," Liam admitted. "We only just got the hang of this one."

"Oh my god, don't," Alice groaned. "The more you talk about this spell, the less confidence I have in you."

Jack smiled ruefully. "Haven't you ever heard of blind trust, oh er-sorry, Alice."

Alice snorted. "Go on then, get on with it," she said to Hayden, who was slowly walking towards her.

This time, they had the foresight to stand shoulder to shoulder, so they didn't end up having to run the length of the room after being shrunk. The coven and Dan soon joined them.

They collectively craned their necks to look up at Cora, who looked horrified and intrigued. "Right," Jack clapped his hands together. "Let's get this show on the road!"

*

They had to while away an hour in the van. Cora had insisted on smuggling them into the van as soon as possible, just to make sure they didn't miss its departure.

"How did anyone not find this van suspicious?" Hayden asked. "It's a white van, with the most thrown together logo on the side, which is obviously a front and it not only operates in the early hours of the morning, but it hangs around for hours before, where anyone could put anything into it," he huffed. "It's like none of them have ever seen a spy thriller in their life before."

Liam laughed. "To be fair, I don't think most people expect themselves to be featuring in a spy thriller. I'm certainly not on the lookout for dodgy behaviour every day of my life."

"Should have brought a card game if we'd thought of it," Hayden said.

"Were you not anticipating a stake out in your spy thriller lifestyle?" Liam teased.

Hayden rolled his eyes. "I wasn't expecting so much sitting around in a spy thriller, that's for certain," he grumbled.

"It's not a bloody film," Dan grumbled. "We get in, get Connor, and get out. No mucking about."

Hayden pulled a face when Dan turned his head.

"We need to help Isadora out, though, right?" Liam asked, "So they stop taking advantage of her? Get her out of her blackmail thing, right?"

"If we get Connor out, he can take his account to the police and that should be enough to raid the place and shut it down. That's the best way to help Ms Pickett," Dan said.

The conversation between the coven and Dan carried on in the background, with Alice occasionally chipping in with protests that she'd come this far and she wasn't going to be left at the gates waiting for them to come back. "I'd be a terrible lookout," she insisted.

Harriet tuned them out and started petting Petal, who was curled up at Alice's feet, asleep. It must have been his longest working day on record, as he'd probably been around the school with Alice during the day, at the shop in the afternoon and now out with them. Harriet wondered if Alice had dog treats in her schoolbag.

Harriet couldn't help but wonder what was happening to Connor at this moment, if he was okay. She couldn't help but wonder if he was suffering less at the hands of their scientific curiosity because of his lack of magic, or if he had been subjected to it more because of the fact that he was a magical anomaly.

She wondered if he would come out of the experience like Ms Pickett had, stripped down and scared, whether Connor would become hardened towards her, Dan and Alice, because they were the reason he'd gotten kidnapped in the first place and they were a glaring reminder, like the coven had been for Ms Pickett. If Connor would regress, deny any supernatural and pretend he was human like he'd thought for so many years as easily as Ms Pickett had regressed back into the comfort of the traditionalist ways she'd been brought up in.

She hadn't known Connor long, a handful of months, which in the scale of her approximately four hundred and fifty years seemed like an inconsequential amount, but some people can shake up your life in such a short time and put a spin on your worldview, and leave you altered at their absence. Harriet had had a similar strength of feeling when she'd first met Cora for the first time, a young angry girl who had demanded the world and in doing so, ironically taught Harriet to think of others. For the first time in a couple hundred years Harriet had someone she was responsible for, especially after she had turned Cora.

Cora always accused her of being too soft and taking in strays, but Cora was the first, and the reason for all the subsequent 'strays', as she called them. Harriet would protest there weren't that many, although maybe that was simply because there weren't many who were still around, either for not being immortal or simply because Harriet and Cora had been forced to move towns to avoid suspicion before the reveal, and they'd lost contact with them.

Simon was the only other who had stayed, a lonely vampire lost in stacks of dusty books that she and Cora had dragged out into the, obviously metaphorical, sunlight to go on adventures. Harriet liked to think he balanced her and Cora's more adventurous natures out quite nicely.

When she met Connor, she knew he was going to be one of Cora's so dubbed 'strays' she took in, simply because he looked so sad, the only human in world of supernatural, trying desperately to fit in despite not knowing what he was himself. Harriet knew she would be friends with him, but she hadn't realised quite how much she had needed Connor as well, someone to remind her what adventuring had felt like after she had given up on having that with Simon and Cora, both of them having grown and gotten jobs, leaving Harriet alone in academia again, still not sure what she wanted to do.

She had hoped that Connor would be one of the ones who stayed for as long as he could, knowing he could only stay for another 60 years probably, and in that time he would grow weaker and be unable to go on adventures, although Harriet doubted that would stop him wanting to.

First, they had to get him out, then she could enjoy the thought of 60 more years of adventuring.

She had briefly considered offering to bite him, but he seemed to have a spark of supernatural about him, and she didn't know how that would interact. She hadn't heard of someone being two different types of supernatural before. Witches had slightly longer lives than humans, like werewolves did, but not much longer. It could mean an extra 20 or 30 years.

The van jolted out of the car park and Harriet out of her thoughts.

"Oh my god," Liam said excitedly. "We're off. It's about time. We're running half an hour late."

Harriet hoped Connor could hang on long enough for them to get there. She was going to get her friend back, come hell or high water.

*

The journey took far less time than the ride there had. When they told Cora they'd been on the motorway, she had been confused, "They must have driven out of town towards Llancallwen and gotten on the dual carriageway, and then come off and circled round back in towards town because it's no more than three miles out. It certainly shouldn't have taken an hour and a half."

It took slightly more time than the 15 minutes that Cora had predicted, quite a bit longer, although nowhere near as long as the ride to HQ. Enough that everyone was starting to get nervous about the timing of this spell wearing off. What kind of traffic was there at nearly five in the morning? Finally, the car slowed, and they heard men talking outside before a buzzing went off and they presumably got through the first layer of security.

Cora hadn't been sure about anything passed this point, "I went to look around the place but just saw the security gates," she'd said, which was about as much as Harriet, Dan and Alice had seen when they'd come to look.

The van stopped.

"Do you think we're here? Is it time to get out?" Liam whispered.

"I don't know," Jack said. "But they better hurry up. We could spell back at any second." There was an edge of worry in his voice that Harriet didn't like. When the guy who was happy to get kidnapped and break into a government facility got nervous, it was time to start freaking out.

There was a banging on the side of the van that made them all jump. "Open her up."

They heard the driver turn the engine off and get out.

"Are they checking the contents before we head in?" Alice asked.

"What do we do?" Several of them hissed, before they all scrambled to get away from the door and hide behind the nearest object. Harriet helped Alice up and directed her to where everyone else was running.

Harriet hoped the sudden tingling in her feet was due to pins and needles and not the indication that the spell was wearing off, although she didn't think luck was on her side.

The van was not a particularly large one but when you're only a few centimetres tall, the sprint to find cover felt like the length of a football pitch. Harriet could hear the footsteps of the driver making his way around the side of the van to open up the rear doors. For every step he took, Harriet's legs were trying to carry her tenfold but were actually only covering a fraction of the distance. It felt like running in dream, when it was like trying to run through water, knowing you should be able to push your legs faster, but they just wouldn't go.

The tingling had reached Harriet's thighs, and she heard somewhere to her left Jack call out, but she couldn't hear what he said.

If Harriet had believed in God, what happened next, in a series of truly unfair events, would be enough to prove not only God's omnipresent existence, but also that he was a completely unsympathetic bugger with a twisted sense of humour.

The tingling in Harriet's legs had reached her neck and before she had the forethought to stop running, she suddenly grew back up to her normal height, but managed to keep her momentum, which meant she crashed into the far wall of the van and sent the entire thing rocking.

Alice, who had been being led by the hand by Harriet, then also grew and crashed into Harriet. They collapsed onto the van floor in a heap and Harriet watched in horror, as one by one, they all grew back to their regular size.

Alice rubbed her head. "You are the worst guide dog ever."

The van, which had previously been stacked high with paper, now also contained six fully grown people and a rather large Labrador, all crammed on top of stacks of paper and each other, as there simply wasn't room anywhere else.

"*What the bloody hell was that?*" came several calls from outside, and the keys rattled in the van doors.

"Uh oh," Jack said as the van doors flew open.

Thankfully, the van must have been in some warehouse or under cover somewhere as no sunlight streamed in. Harriet was grateful, mostly because she hadn't thought to grab her umbrella in her initial rush to get to the back of the van, and it was now sat somewhere by the doors, with five people and a dog between them.

"*Who the hell are you lot?*" came the angry voice from the door, and the sound of several guns cocking.

There was no response from their group, although in their defence they had just all had the wind knocked out of them.

She sighed and asked the livid man at the door, "Would you mind passing me my umbrella?"

Chapter Twenty-One

Harriet wasn't sure what they'd been zapped with, or injected with, or even more simply hit over the head with, but she remembered getting pulled out of the van one by one, and then she woke up in a cell.

Her head wasn't thumping, so she doubted they'd been clocked over the head, although she hadn't had much blood recently. It could be that there simply wasn't enough to cause a substantial bruise and an accompanying head throb.

Harriet could see Dan across from her. He was sat upright and on his phone. She was surprised they'd allowed him to keep that.

"How did you hang on to that one?" Harriet asked, and her mouth felt dry. She propped herself up against the wall. Her umbrella had been placed on the floor next to her, which surprised her again. Although there were no windows in the cells anyway, they were probably at basement level at the minute.

"I stuck it in my pants," Dan said, without looking up from the phone "How's your head?"

"In your—my head's fine. Did they knock us unconscious?" Harriet asked.

"No, they swung open one of the doors into the back of your head after we got out the van. It was accidental," Dan said, "And I hid my phone in my pants in the hopes they'd only check my pockets, which they did."

"Why not your sock?" Harriet said. She couldn't believe she'd been knocked out by military men with guns at a top-secret facility and it had been because of a wayward door. What kind of badass story was that?

"I didn't think of that," Dan said, looking up from his phone for the first time.

"So where are the others? Are they in another cell?" Harriet asked, although she couldn't hear anything coming from any of the nearby cells. There was only a few, maybe six in total, and she could only see one other one in use, although due to the angle they were sitting at in their cell, she could only see their legs.

"Harriet," Dan said, as if she was particularly dim witted, "We entered a base kidnapping magic users, with a witch whose blindness has made other aspects of her magic stronger than the average witch and three male witches who grew up within spitting distance of each other, despite the fact there's less than a thousand recorded existing in the UK. We basically handed them several magical anomalies on a plate."

"So, they've taken them into the lab," Harriet said. This was exactly what deep down, they knew was going to happen. Harriet had just hoped Alice wasn't going to be one of them. The coven were old enough to make their own stupid choices and at least had a rough idea of what was going on in the labs 20 years ago, and they'd still agreed, knowing the risks. Alice was a teenager, and as much as she pushed passed being blind as a restriction, it certainly wasn't going to help her escape on her own.

Harriet groaned and slammed her head back into the wall behind her.

"For God's sake, what are we going to do?" Harriet said, annoyed that Dan was already back on his phone.

"Well, I'm contacting my pack and letting them know I've been taken prisoner and I've also contacted the police," Dan said, putting his phone away. Thankfully, in his pocket this time.

"So, help is on the way?"

"Yes. The police have reasonable grounds to enter now that they have evidence of a hostage situation. Although Officer Wellard is not happy with us, just fair warning," Dan said, with a small grin.

"So, it actually worked?" Harriet asked, feeling oddly bereft. "The police are on their way, this place is getting shut down, and we just need to wait for the cavalry to arrive? And then back home in time for breakfast?" It all felt incredibly anticlimactic.

"All because the no homo military boys didn't want to stick their hands down my pants," Dan smirked.

"Yay for heteronormativity, I guess?" Harriet said.

"What's the matter? You seem weirdly unexcited that everything worked out. Were you hoping for more explosions?" Dan asked, his standard one eyebrow raised in judgement.

"It just doesn't make sense," Harriet huffed. She wasn't quite sure how to describe what she was feeling, so she hoped if she continued speaking for long enough, the words would suddenly form to perfectly describe how she felt. "Mr Jones, why would he want to build a research facility that kidnapped witches *and* demons. Surely that doesn't make sense. Like, why would he need to investigate demons. Surely he already knows everything and what he doesn't know he could ask another demon that he knows?"

Dan shrugged, "Ms Pickett told us he was wrapped up in it all, and it was his fault she got involved in the first place. So, we know he had at least some hand in it and Cora positively ID'd him. I don't know. You have to prepare yourself for the possibility that he might actually be responsible for this."

"Why did he get shot then?"

"Decoy? To make people think he was the innocent one, the victim. He's set it up so if the company went under, he'd looked like one of the blackmailed foot soldiers," Dan said, although Harriet got the feeling there was no real conviction behind his words. He felt it too, the idea niggling at the back of her mind that things didn't add up.

"And why would he have beer mats with the victims' names and numbers in his house?"

"Maybe he still went and collected some victims himself, to keep his cover? There's CCTV at the bar. It could be his alibi," Harriet got the feeling Dan was merely playing Devil's advocate at this point.

"Cora said he ran a few businesses. He wouldn't have the time he would have had to hire someone for that," Harriet argued.

"I don't know," Dan said, sounding more unsure.

"And then what about the letters me and Connor found at his house? Thanking him from his contributions? Why would he send letters to himself on the off chance some students broke into his flat?" Harriet said, her thoughts were starting to come together now, and it was becoming clear that certain things didn't add up when it came to Mr Jones being responsible for the lab. It was far more likely that Mr Jones actually was a blackmailed foot soldier.

"I think the damning question," a voice said from behind her, "is if he were in charge of the operation, why would he be sat in a cell behind you?"

Harriet swung round. The pair of legs that had only been visible previously had shuffled forward in their cell to reveal Mr Jones' new body, with presumably Mr Jones inside it.

"Mr Jones?" Harriet and Dan said, in joint disbelief.

"What the hell are you doing here?" Harriet asked.

"Well," Mr Jones said, sounding haggard and not like his usually jovial self. Harriet wondered how long he'd been here, "I threatened to go to the police with what was happening and so they shot me. I'm sure you remember that part, got one of their military men I believe," he directed at Harriet. "However, when I went to the police station for questioning about the shooting, I said I had information about these disappearances, but I wanted to go into witness protection in exchange. It took far longer than anticipated so I stayed in police custody."

"That's why you got held up. It wasn't police prejudice at all. You were whistle blowing," Harriet said.

"Yes, and then the police said someone came into the station. A student, kicking up a fuss about me being held illegally. May I presume that was you?" Mr Jones asked.

"That was Connor, actually." Mr Jones looked confused. "Connor Manning. He was in Pickett's class,"

"Well, I admire his loyalty, considering I'd never met the boy. However, the police weren't sure if it was one of this lot," he gestured to the cells, "Who'd found out, checking to see if I was still with the police, so they hurried me along, fast tracked everything and I was meant to depart that evening."

"And then you got kidnapped?" Harriet said.

Mr Jones nodded, "Them shooting me was my warning to stop. After it became clear I had spoken to the police, they brought me here,"

"Have they been experimenting on you?" Harriet asked; he'd been here for at least a month.

"No," Mr Jones sounded as curious as Harriet felt. "I've been expecting it. They always threatened it if we didn't keep our mouths closed, we'd be next. Of course, there was financial gain too, so their arses were covered if all got revealed. No one was going to believe we were blackmailed if we'd gotten paid."

Harriet was stumped. What Mr Jones was saying sounded reasonable, and it made as much sense as anything else. It did leave one question unanswered though.

"So, who's running this place, then? Who was your boss?" Harriet asked.

"I don't know," Mr Jones said, looking defeated. "We never got put in contact with the 'big man upstairs'," he said sarcastically. "Just sent one of his military men to give us our orders, and we'd report back to them. We were told to pitch it as a job opportunity when we spoke to the girls," he sounded sick of himself as he spoke. "A lot of them had fallen out with their covens or were on the verge of getting kicked out. We were told to tell them they could have a place here with other witches in the same position."

"And the demons?" Harriet asked quietly.

"The loners, the down-and-out types." Mr Jones added quietly, "The ones no one would miss."

Harriet couldn't say she was happy Mr Jones wasn't the main man in charge, because yes, it meant he didn't orchestrate the sick idea, but he still had a hand in making it work. He still sold out others to keep himself safe. Harriet had sworn blind to Pickett that she would never have sent people in instead of her to one of these labs, and Harriet had known she'd been right about Ms Pickett, that witches were a self-serving lot, distrusting and cruel, but maybe Harriet had simply been playing into her own prejudices. She had been astounded to hear about Mr Jones being caught up in anything dodgy, finding it inconceivable that he'd be running it, because he always seemed so honest. He believed in the sharing of knowledge like Harriet did, understood like all vampires and demons did about mankind's record throughout history, that their history that was covered in blood and then covered up, had also been scathing of humanity's hypocrisy. She couldn't help but feel a kinship to him. Harriet didn't want to believe Mr Jones threw others on the fire in front of himself, because it was easy to believe you would never do it yourself when comparing to your polar opposite, but when someone so like you in opinion and experience does the exact thing you had both rallied against, you couldn't help but examine whether truly you would hold to your own beliefs in such a circumstance.

Nobody likes to think themselves capable of such things, but Harriet was starting to realise that the fact of the matter was that no matter whether you were human, or what kind of supernatural you were, everybody was a self-serving asshole at heart, and it was only how well they hid it that varied. It was a depressingly cynical thought, and she was already in a fairly morbid situation.

"I've had a thought," Dan said, sounding hesitant. "You're not going to like it."

Harriet raised an eyebrow questioningly. She'd just had a particularly unpleasant thought. She didn't know if she wanted another one.

"Well, there's only one reason that we initially thought Mr Jones was heading this lab, and that's because of what Cora said. And now we know Mr Jones isn't running it, it does beg the question why Cora said it was him." Dan seemed to brace himself.

Harriet refused to consider what Dan was entertaining, "Her boss probably just looks like Mr Jones, besides, she said he was a demon, right? He might have made himself look like Mr Jones on purpose, so he could use him as a scapegoat."

"I don't know any Cora?" Mr Jones said, and more helpfully added, "Nor have I heard anyone round her mention her name. Plus, the boss is a man. I've definitely heard the guards referring to 'he' and 'him'.."

"See? She probably just got the guys mixed up," Harriet said, closing down Dan's line of inquiry.

"Okay but, Cora said she was speaking to the police, right? And we figured she was the police's 'source' that they had. Well, we know that's Mr Jones now, so why did she lie?" Dan argued, determined not to let this go.

"Police can have two sources of information," Harriet said.

"I never heard them mention a second source," Mr Jones said. Harriet glared at him. He was complicit in the kidnapping of several underage girls; what did he know?

"But doesn't it make more sense? Mr Jones couldn't give them any more information because he got kidnapped and that's when their investigation ground to a halt. Cora said she's been talking to them for the last few weeks, but if she had, they would have had grounds to investigate by now."

"Why are you so intent on it being her? Besides, the boss is a man," Harriet spat back at Dan.

"Why is it so hard to believe that she could have gotten caught up and blackmailed like Jones and Pickett?" Dan stood his ground. Despite the fact they were both still sitting, they looked like toddlers having a fight.

"Well, how would you like it if I said Madison was volunteering here on weekends. You'd sure as hell leap to her defence. How is it any different?"

"You have to at least consider it as a possibility. Cora wasn't fond of witches, you could tell, but I don't think anyone in the supernatural community who isn't a witch themselves likes them. They're like the collective supernatural asshole. No one is going to hold it against her but is it so hard to believe someone used that dislike and twisted it for their own use?"

"She's two hundred years old, not a child. You don't have to patronise her!"

"Just think how defiant she was about us not coming here."

"She was scared for us!"

"An action can have two motives. Just, just don't think of her as Cora, just another person, any other person, and look at the facts. I've been thinking about this. She said initially she knew the building and the logo, and would dig up information for us, which she never did—"

"She was busy," Harriet interrupted stubbornly.

"Also," Dan spoke louder. "You kept her up to date on everything we were doing, right? That's how they knew we were sneaking into the club with Jack and that's why we got taken to HQ, and then a van goes every week but ours was the one to get stopped? She pretended to help us when she knew she couldn't convince us to leave it, and so she made sure we got caught before we could sneak in." Dan looked her hard in the eyes, "It makes sense, you have to admit it."

"I don't want to," Harriet said quietly.

"I know, but you have to be prepared for what's going to happen when the police get here," Dan said, his voice dropping to a gentle, comforting tone.

Harriet realised that the police weren't going to go easy on those who had been complicit, especially if Cora actually hadn't been feeding information to the police. Harriet straightened herself up and started examining the corridor, pressing her face up as closely to the bars as she could. Dan looked worried that she'd gone off into the deep end.

Harriet was just doing what any pseudo-sibling with maternal instincts would do, she was going to go and clear up her pseudo-sibling's mess and get her out of trouble.

"Do the guards carry the keys on their belts?" Harriet asked Mr Jones, who was looking at her with unrestrained and unwanted pity.

"Yes, it's not so much a key, though, as an electronic fob. All the guards should have one."

"Perfect," Harriet grinned and started yelling as loudly as she could.

"What are you doing?" Dan asked. "The police will be here in minutes, just sit tight,"

"Not a chance. If, and that's a big if, if Cora is caught up in this somehow, she's gonna tell me about it before the police get involved. You know how incompetent the police are." Harriet started yelling again, and she heard one of the guards opening a door down the corridor.

She grinned, her elongated teeth on full display.

"Pass me my umbrella. We're breaking out of this joint." She grinned.

Dan rolled his eyes at the dramatics, but passed over her umbrella and stood, prepared for whatever was about to happen next with a grim expression.

Chapter Twenty-Two

Harriet was amazed at how easy it was to lure the guard close enough that Dan got his arms through the bars and hands around the guard's throat, and then how easy it was to swipe the magnetic key from his belt and unlock their cell.

Dan headbutted the guard and knocked him unconscious. Harriet rolled her eyes at the dramatic show.

"You could have just locked him in the cell," Harriet said.

Dan shrugged. "He could have yelled for help. Easier this way."

"And it looked badass," Mr Jones argued. Dan looked oddly proud of himself.

Harriet rolled her eyes at the pair of them. "Come on," she muttered.

Harriet and Dan started down the corridor, and Mr Jones called out, "Aren't you going to let me out?"

"No," Harriet turned back, still making her way towards the exit. "It'll help your alibi when the police get here if you're locked up. Besides, you helped kidnap at least nine young girls. You're not forgiven."

Dan just kind of shrugged at Mr Jones in a way that said, 'She's not wrong', before he took off after her down the corridor.

*

"Wait!" Dan said, and Harriet slowed her pace. She could see the guards' station at the end of the corridor. They just needed to get past that before they could get to the main building.

"These are the magical suppression cells," Dan said, pointing to a set of double doors with a piece of paper taped to the doors reading 'Magical Suppression Cells'.

"They really pulled out all the stops," Harriet scoffed.

146

"They might keep the prisoners in here. We should check it out." Dan already had one hand on the door, pushing it ajar. Harriet hadn't considered they'd be kept in cells. When the labs had originally opened, they were like hospital wards, only with security men and barred windows. It was how humans justified it being humane. Harriet had assumed whoever was orchestrating this was going to model it off the previous labs, but she supposed it you were already doing it illegally, there was no need to justify anything being humane.

Harriet dithered between wanting to find Connor and everyone else and wanting to find Cora before the police arrived and get her side of the story before the police twisted it and botched the whole thing.

"Fine," she said, because she had no idea if Cora was even in the building, but there was a strong chance that everyone else was behind the two doors.

Harriet and Dan burst through with all the dramatic bravos of a movie star in an action film. All that was missing was a declaration of 'Aha!'. Although any such declaration would have been premature as Harriet and Dan stood in the corridor with empty cells on both sides.

Once again, there were six cells in total, just as it was in the regular cells, the only difference being the lack of Mr Jones, and the fact the doors were a different colour, clearly in whatever metal it was the cells needed to suppress magic. Harriet couldn't remember the exact metal, but she knew it had to be infused with magic to work.

"There's no one here," Dan said blankly.

"Let's go," Harriet said, heading back towards the door, "Right, we need to get past the guards station. ETA on the police?"

Dan looked at the time on his phone, "Should literally be any second."

"Okay, we need to be quick then," Harriet had to find whatever the boss had blackmailed Cora with and destroy it before the police arrived.

Harriet went to walk through the door. She figured she could come up with a plan on route, and if not, hit and run was always there as a backup.

"Wait," Dan said, pulling her back through the door, just as a guard rounded the corner.

"Wha—"

"Sh!" Dan and Harriet held their breath as they waited for the guard to pass and head back towards the way they came, towards the regular cells. "He's going to check on the other guard, said he's taking too long, which means there's only one guard at the station at the minute. Now's our best shot."

They both made a break for the station. Dan was right, there was only one guard left at the station. He was almost bald, the few brown hairs that clung to his head were matted down with sweat. He was lazing at the desk, and even when he saw the vampire and werewolf sprinting directly towards him, he didn't stand up. His eyes widened and he let out a strangled yell for help, which was cut off mid-yelp when Harriet punched him straight in the face. His head bounced off the wall behind him and he slumped unconscious on the desk.

Dan raised an eyebrow at her, but they both took off around the corner before the second guard came back.

Harriet shrugged. "One guard each. Figured it was fair that way."

Dan snorted. "We've got a couple of minutes before the second one gets back and sounds whatever alarm system they've got here."

"Right," Harriet said. They came up to a flight of stairs, which led up to the back of the building, off the main entrance. "Where now?"

"Keep going up," Dan said, without breaking stride. "No one ever keeps anything top secret on the ground floor, in case it jumps out the window."

Harriet figured that made sense.

When they got to the first floor, there was a handy map of the building opposite the stairwell. Harriet was surprised they hadn't come across more security. Anyone would think it actually was a university.

Dan pointed to the map. "It says 'Rooms' are the floor above. Reckon they're there?"

Harriet looked at the map. Above the rooms, there was a 'Recreation and Canteen' floor, and above that was the chilling 'Laboratories', which Harriet wanted to claw off the map with her nails just for the satisfaction of erasing it. Finally, above that floor was the top floor, which read 'Head Office'. Harriet figured that was her best shot at finding if Cora was involved.

"I'm going to the top. I have to find out if Cora helped with any of this."

Dan didn't look happy, but he looked resigned, as if he knew he wasn't going to be able to talk her out of it. "Fine. I'm going to find Connor."

Harriet nodded. They made their way up the next flight of stairs before Dan ran off further into the building and Harriet continued her way up the stairs. She was wishing she'd had more blood before she left, as her lungs weren't taking in as much oxygen as she needed. She was loath to use the elevators, though, she'd seen enough action movies to know when the elevators door opened on the floor you needed, there were always security men with guns waiting on the other side and you were trapped. She supposed she could use her umbrella as a flimsy battering ram, or something to the like, but she still preferred to take the stairs.

By the time she reached the right floor, Harriet was paranoid she was going to come across security guards, considering the lack of them she'd come across so far.

None appeared when she poked her head out of the stairwell, so she made her way over to the map on the wall. As well as the descriptors for each floor, there was a detailed map of each one. Harriet glanced at the small layout of the rooms on the second floor and wondered if Dan had found anyone by now.

The map for this floor was enlarged, and showed a string of offices, including a councillor's officer for some reason, but at the end of the corridor, furthest from where Harriet was, was the boss' office, because wasn't that always the way? Harriet rolled her eyes at her own damn luck and set off down the corridor, thankful for the line of closed doors on either side of the corridor, which meant the corridor was only lit by the overhead lights and she could close her umbrella.

The corridor was long and straight, and Harriet had the odd urge for a bike, as the corridor as it stood seemed endless.

When she reached the end of the corridor, it had only taken several minutes, she realised why the entire place had a hollowed out feeling to it. It was still only half six in the morning, Harriet had gotten the impression that it was still day due to the sun, but she'd forgotten that most humans still weren't up at this time.

The door loomed at the end of the corridor, squaring off the offices as it sat at a dead end.

Harriet hesitantly twisted the door handle. She wasn't sure if she wanted the boss to be behind it or not. She wanted to confront him, and she at least had the knowledge that if he held her there that the police should be showing up any minute and she wouldn't be held for any length of time. Not like her friends who had probably been experimented on, like the young teenage girls had been held here for months, who knew what horrors they'd faced already.

It was that thought that steeled Harriet's resolve, and she flung the door open, umbrella held out in case there was an open window.

When Harriet realised there were no windows in the office and it was only lit by the light fixture above, she started to lower her umbrella. She had the fleeting thought that the whole building seemed oddly vampire friendly, when the umbrella lowered enough that she saw who was sat behind the desk.

An incredibly sheepish Cora, who looked on the verge of tears. "Let me explain."

Chapter Twenty-Three

"Look, whatever they're blackmailing you with, I'll get you out, okay?" Harriet said, holding her hands up and walking slowly towards the desk, as if Cora were about to blow. Cora's lip trembled.

"I didn't mean for you to get caught. I tried to get you to stay away," Cora said, her voice hiccupping with the force of keeping her tears at bay, her cheeks were flushed and her eyes were red rimmed, she looked as human as when Harriet had first met her. Harriet idly thought she must have had a lot of blood recently to be able to cry in the first place.

"Whatever it is, we'll move again. The police won't go after you, I promise. They'll know you were blackmailed. I doubt they would even attempt to track you down," Harriet said, not sure if what she was saying was true, but she knew she wouldn't let any of them near Cora. She could possibly even persuade Simon to move, and the three of them would start all over again, like old times. She would have to leave Connor and her newly formed friendships with Dan and Alice, but it would be worth it for her little family. Dan would do the same for his pack, and Alice for her coven. Connor would understand too, she knew he would. She'd be able to come back and see him when the heat had died down.

"No," Cora whispered, her voice wobbling.

"What?"

Cora just shook her head; tears had started streaking down her cheeks, staining her face.

"I promise, you won't get in trouble. You were blackmailed, for god's sake! I'll take care of everything." Harriet dared take another step closer to the desk, almost touching her side of it, but Cora flung her hands out, and just choked out the word 'no' a few times, until Harriet retreated back a step.

"What's wrong?" Harriet asked, "We need to hurry, the police are arriving any second. They might already be here,"

Cora just slumped, "It's over."

"That's right," Harriet said. Hopefully, Cora would come with her sooner rather than later. Harriet couldn't hear anything that indicated the police had arrived, but they might still be several floors down.

"No, the company is over. I failed," Cora sobbed. She slumped onto the desk.

"What do you mean? The facility is shutting down. That's good."

"You don't understand," Cora said through gritted teeth, trying to hold back more tears. "It's my company. I started it and I've failed."

Harriet shook her head, "No, you—you're the boss' PA, and you got blackmailed into helping him. Why else would you do this?" Harriet's stomach was somewhere around her knees.

"Hundreds and hundreds of years of male oppression and you think I'm going to settle being someone's PA?" Cora said scathingly.

Harriet couldn't help resort to snapping, "Don't exaggerate, you're barely passed two hundred." Harriet didn't want to think what it meant, that Cora had been the one to organise kidnapping all of those girls. She couldn't have. "No." Harriet said, "No, everyone said the boss was male, that everyone referred to him as male. Are you covering for him?"

"No," Cora snapped. "I created this entire company. I did everything. There is no man. The security and the scouters think I'm a man because they were more frightened by and willing to obey a man. It was easier to keep everyone in line."

"What's the point in being a modern businesswoman if everyone thinks you're a man!" Harriet shouted. She couldn't believe Cora had been so stupid; she'd gotten herself in too deep, chasing after the dream of owning a business.

"Trust me!" Cora shouted back, she leapt from her chair and stared Harriet down, her jaw gritted and eyes furious. "Sometimes you have to sacrifice things. If I proved I could do this right, I wouldn't have to pretend to be a man next time."

"Prove to who? These are people's lives you're talking about!" Harriet wanted to claw at her hair in frustration, but she stared Cora down instead.

"Look, I'll let your friends go. I'll destroy their data. Just give me time to sort this place out. I can make it better," Cora pleaded.

Harriet felt sick, "The police are already on their way and they might be here already for all I know." Harriet felt tears pricking her own eyes, although she'd not drunk enough blood for the tears to fall. "How could you? It's illegal, not to mention completely immoral," her voice was barely above a whisper.

"It's not illegal, it's government funded! And no one is here against their will, everyone volunteered!" Cora insisted, rather angrily.

"You kidnapped them!" Harriet bit back.

"No, we didn't!"

"You kidnapped them from bars."

"No," Cora said firmly, as if she were the one in the moral right. "We talked to people who were at odds with their covens, about to become homeless, young girls those covens were going to leave on the streets to fend for themselves! We offered them a home and food, and all they had to do was help us understand, give us information, so we could learn about magic, that even the supernatural community doesn't know about!"

"So, the government got you to find out, because it wanted intel on magic? Labs are illegal."

"This isn't a lab," Cora said slowly and with menace, as if Harriet were a dense child. "We offered young witches a place to stay, offered to get rid of demons debts if they helped. It's not a lab, it's research facility. No one is here against their will."

"They volunteered under duress because they had no other alternative! That's not a choice, it's not moral," Harriet said, couldn't believe how much the government had twisted her mind on this. She was delusional.

"No," Cora said softly, "We don't torture people, or experiment. It's like—like a clinical trial. It's all above board standard. We don't do anything they don't agree to, otherwise we wouldn't be allowed to keep this place open."

"Then why is everything being handled as if it's illegal?" Harriet asked, not believing for a second that this place wasn't exactly like the labs from twenty years ago.

"Because there were some legal loopholes that the government went through to get this place open, and so we haven't been able to make it public. That's why none of the participants could have access to the outside, and why none of the scouters knew fully what was happening. We couldn't risk it getting out in case we got shut down. We were going to go public eventually," Cora said, as if she were trying to persuade Harriet. "Once we had concrete results coming in, until then if humans found out, we would have been shut down in seconds so everyone could pat themselves on the back and say they'd done good. But if you showed humans concrete findings about how magic works, and then told them it was from a volunteer lab, humans can see the benefit, and are then weirdly okay with it. If you show humans how it directly benefits them and their safety, they will forgive something they'd previously been dead against."

"What does the government want with the information?" Harriet wondered if Alice's musing about magic warfare had more truth to it than they previously thought. Even if Cora's heart was in the right place, the government's certainly wasn't. "What about Mr Jones? You shot him, for god's sake!" Harriet said. There was no chance they were above board, or ever going to go public. Although Harriet couldn't see why Cora would be lying now.

"We knew he wouldn't die. It was a warning shot. He was going to blow the whistle. That's why he's been held downstairs, until everything is already out."

"Why not include him in your trials?"

"Because he didn't want to. He didn't believe us when we said it wasn't like the old labs, so we haven't used him. I told you, nothing happens that the volunteer doesn't okay,"

"But he's not allowed to leave! And what about Connor? He wasn't kicked out of a coven or has loads of debt. What could you have possibly told him?"

"Actually, we did offer to pay off his student debt, but he just wanted to know what the hell he was when the scout approached him in the bar and offered him the job opportunity. He just wanted us to help him find out what he is."

"So, he came voluntarily?" Harriet asked, and Cora nodded. She was going to have to kill Connor, although she had a feeling Dan might get to him first.

"But you blackmailed the scouters," Harriet insisted, despite the fact that Connor had volunteered, Mr Jones and Ms Pickett certainly hadn't.

"Only the top circle of management and the scientists know what really goes on here, security and all the footmen are just leased out from a company," Cora said, and Harriet felt bad for punching that guard earlier now she knew he didn't know what was happening. "So, all the scouters knew was what they worked out. We hired them because they were local. They frequented the magic bar and they wanted to earn extra cash. We hired about twenty of them. Ms Pickett only got threatened so badly because she stumbled on Jones and was a liability, so we had to make sure she and Jones didn't conspire to shut us down because they thought they'd worked out what we were doing. So we threatened them, because they were far more likely to believe their suspicions to be true than that we weren't doing what they thought," Cora sighed, and slumped against the desk. "It all started spiralling after that. Things kept going wrong and I had to lie more and more to keep everything covered, and then you got involved and I had to lie to you." Cora sounded so defeated.

"You're upset you lied to me," Harriet said, having a revelation, "But you're not upset about what you've done."

"No," Cora said softly, "because I've not done anything wrong. Sure, things got slightly out of hand with threats and lying, but nothing I've done is illegal, nothing immoral, just a bit dodgy and maybe a tad dubious. Everyone here volunteered, just like your friend Connor, because we were helping them in some way.

"We helped them test the limits of their magic in a controlled environment, so many of their covens kept them from testing anything new, we encourage them to try whatever they like. The whole place is led by the individual. It's all about knowledge here." Cora said passionately. "Isn't that your favourite quote?" She smiled knowingly, "'Knowledge shouldn't be constrained by the few, to disadvantage the masses', Professor Lewis used to say that, didn't he? That's what this was about, all of it. I promise."

Harriet wanted to argue. It was still wrong morally. "Why didn't you just pay the volunteers then, like a proper clinical trial?"

"Because they couldn't have contact with the outside world once they'd signed up. Not at first, anyway. What use was paying them? They didn't want paying."

Harriet couldn't fault that, she supposed.

"I insisted on this being about knowledge when the government first suggested it. They wanted to make it about learning about magic so they could defend themselves against it, but I fought bloody hard to make it what it is. The whole motto of this place is 'Knowledge itself is power' because of what *you* taught me. You're the one who taught me to always seek knowledge even if it's being withheld from me, and now it's going to get torn down!"

"Cora," Harriet said softly, "You still need to leave." Harriet knew no matter whether she agreed with what Cora had done morally, the police weren't going to stop and chat with her about it. She had known Cora for almost all of Cora's 227 years of life, felt responsible for her and she couldn't give her up, no matter what had happened between them.

"You saved me from my family," Cora said quietly into the room, looking down at the desk in front of her rather than at Harriet. "You saved me, and gave me a new home, and sure, your actions then may have been considered self-defence by some, but your actions were morally dubious at best, but you knew yourself that it was the right thing to do. How is what I'm doing different? I'm helping witches, and demons seek knowledge, giving them a home off the streets or relieving them of debt, and sure, while it's dodgy, the government using legal loopholes and hiding it from the public, I know myself that what I'm doing is right, and I want you to trust me." Cora looked at Harriet, "Please."

Harriet didn't respond. She knew she was going to end up trusting Cora despite what her better judgment said. Harriet knew that Cora was right, she had trusted Harriet when Harriet said her actions were for the best, and now it was time to put the same trust back into Cora. Harriet still had the dual desire to protect Cora from everything, because she was her responsibility, but she had to trust her and she wanted to. It didn't mean her emotions weren't battling each other, though.

"It doesn't matter what I think, it's over," Harriet said back quietly. "The police should be here by now, unless they're even more incompetent than previously thought. Dan must have called them an hour ago."

"I just need to leave," Cora said, as if out of all topics covered so far, this was the one she had been avoiding. "When this out comes out, and it will, the government will look for a scapegoat, to cover public image, so I need to disappear for a while."

Harriet nodded. Although she'd already figure that was the case, she still felt her heart drop. She'd been planning on going with Cora originally. She didn't think that was the case this time.

"I can come back when it's all blown over," Cora promised.

"I'll come looking for you," Harriet promised back.

Cora gave a small smile of relief, as if she hadn't been expecting that response. "Too curious for my own good I'm afraid," which had always been Harriet and Cora's defence to Simon when he'd found they'd done something reckless.

"Just two curious, headstrong women," Harriet recounted back, and Cora grinned.

"Thank you," she whispered, before she made her way out of the door, and off into the building.

Harriet wondered how long it would be before she saw her friend again.

Chapter Twenty-Four

Harriet sprinted down the stairs. She needed to meet back up with Dan and see if he'd found the others. She figured she would be best to look for him where she'd left him. By the time she got back down to the second floor, she could hear the wailing of sirens and the shouts of resistance, indicating both that the police had arrived, and that the staff were not accepting it.

Harriet had to duck behind several objects as men in uniforms rushed past her, shouting. She was having a hard time telling who were police and who were security guards as their uniforms were only subtly different. Although Harriet figured as she'd broken into the building and was therefore trespassing, she was probably not going to be liked by either group and it was probably best to avoid them both.

Once the group of men had run past, Harriet took off in the opposite direction, heading towards the rooms that had been indicated on the map earlier. There seemed to have been an entire block of them. Harriet wondered how many supernaturals had actually been kidnapped, or had volunteered, she mentally corrected. How many more Cora had been planning to recruit.

Harriet knew that Cora was not a bad person, but could definitely make stupid decisions, as could everyone. She felt emotionally gutted that her friend had needed to leave, and she wasn't sure when she was going to see her again. Harriet knew it was for the best, though, and she had eternity to meet up with her friend. It would come around sooner or later.

Harriet shook her doubts as she crept into the wing that must have housed the volunteers. She'd also discovered why they were no vampire spies, as it was hard to look inconspicuous when wielding a large black umbrella. Thankfully, in a truly dire situation, it could be used to knock somebody unconscious with, so she felt this evened things out.

She had managed to make her way through a large recreation room with consoles and a pool table, and some large cushy sofas. Apparently, Connor had been living it up here. There were apartment buildings in the city that were less nicely furnished than here, and it was certainly a step up from student accommodation.

When she continued through the large double doors, she noted that there seemed to be individual rooms, rather than one large hospital like ward. This was looking like everyone had their own private room. Harriet peered into one, and it had a single bed, a window (thankfully with the blinds drawn), an en suite and plenty of mess that indicated individuals were allowed to bring their own possessions and decorate their rooms to their own liking. It wasn't that Harriet hadn't believed Cora when she said it was different to how the labs had previously been, but it was nice to have it confirmed.

"Harriet?" came a voice behind her. She spun and raised her umbrella menacingly.

"Oh, Dan," she sighed in relief, lowering the umbrella, and then noticed who was standing next to him. "Connor!" She sprinted at him, dropping her umbrella on route and hugging him strongly. "We've missed you." She let him go, took a long look at his face and then cuffed him around the head. "You moron! You came here voluntarily. We thought you'd been kidnapped. We were worried sick about what was happening to you."

Connor looked sheepish, "Sorry, I was gonna call, but they said no outside contact for a while. I was just telling these guys about it." He gestured to Dan and the coven, who Dan had also clearly found.

Dan looked annoyed at Connor for his lapse in better judgement, but his glare was slightly undercut by the soft, relieved look on his face.

"Okay, you found these guys. Where's Alice?" Harriet said, suddenly noting the young girl wasn't among their ranks.

"We're just looking for her," Dan said, at the same time Jack said, "He didn't find us. We busted out."

Dan rolled his eyes. "I followed the explosion and found you. Apparently, she's most likely to be in the girls' wing."

"It's this way," Connor said, before taking off down the corridor. The others scrambled after him.

"We need to be careful," Harriet called, slightly behind after she had to fumble on the ground for her umbrella. She'd made it this far without being burned to a crisp. She'd like to see if she could make it back out of the government facility the same way. "The police don't know who's staff and who's kidnapped. They're going to be taking everyone in," Harriet said, when she finally caught up to Connor and Dan at the front. They'd finally slowed down as they reached a junction in the corridors.

"No one was kidnapped, though. The staff are fine," Connor said.

"The police don't know that. They were called in the deal with a kidnap and potential hostage situation with an illegal government agency. You think they're going to stop and ask questions?" Harriet said.

Connor and Dan nodded and conceded her point.

"Plus," Dan said, "If Wellard is here and he finds us, he's not going to be happy that we broke in after he specifically said not to. Best we try and get out without getting detained by the police."

Connor nodded, "Trespassing charges do look bad on job applications."

Dan suddenly pushed them back, "Hide. There's a group of people heading this way." They all ducked into an unlocked room to the side of them, which was another one of the private rooms, thankfully empty.

"Where are all of the volunteers?" Harriet asked. She hadn't seen anyone who didn't look like police or staff running around.

Connor shrugged. "A group took off towards the rec room when the police arrived, but I think that was because most of the demons here are here to get gambling debts wiped or loans repaid that they're late on. They're a twitchy bunch when the police come knocking."

Liam nodded, "When we broke out, we passed a load of witches that were convinced their covens had called the police to track them down. I think most of them are hiding."

"Why did you have to break out? None of the doors are locked," Connor asked.

Jack gave a wide-eyed innocent look that Harriet didn't buy for a second, "Didn't test to see if it was locked. We just blew up the door."

"Oops," Hayden deadpanned. Connor laughed.

Dan hushed them as the footsteps grew louder, and there were frantic voices bickering back and forth about legality, until one said, "I can't get brought home by the police again. My wife will kill me. She already thinks I must be manufacturing methamphetamines or something."

"Stop volunteering for secret government schemes then, they always get shut down! Don't know why I followed you here," the voice trailed off and they continued down the hall.

Connor whispered, "That has to be Benny and Will. They're two of the lab technicians who work here. They're a right laugh."

Harriet suddenly startled into realising that while Connor hadn't been tortured while he was here, the whole reason he'd come was because he'd wanted his own questions answered. "Did they work out what you are?"

Dan looked startled, as if Connor hadn't told him the reason he had been 'kidnapped' in the first place. The coven looked confused. "I thought you said he was a witch?" Jack asked. Harriet paused at his tone, wondering if they'd been planning to ask Connor to join them.

"Yeah, they did. They were dead confused at first, but then I started talking to Neil, who's a demon here, been around for ages, and he said—" Dan clapped his hand over Connor mouth as another group of footsteps grew closer, and then faded again, heading in the same direction that Benny and Will had gone.

"Quick version?" Dan said to Connor, glancing at the door, as if more people were on the way.

"I'm half-demon," Connor said, equally put out at being hurried, but also bursting with excitement to tell them.

"A what?" most of them asked in unison.

"So, Neil was saying that when demons first started making bodies, some of them made them exactly as humans are, with all the biology and everything. The majority didn't bother because it was a hassle, but some did because they thought it was the easiest way not to get caught and my mum must have been one of them, as it wasn't common to make the bodies, let alone settle down with a human and get pregnant. They reckon there can't be more than one or two of us in the UK."

"So, what does that mean? Can you use it for anything?" Harriet asked.

Connor shrugged. "That was the next round of testing, but they reckon I've probably got an extended lifespan and I'm most likely a bit more robust than you've average human. They didn't think I'd be able to properly possess someone because I'm tied to this body, but we were going to test some other stuff. No wonder Alice's witch classes weren't working," Connor grinned. It was a wide smile, one of someone who'd finally worked out the answer to a riddle after a ridiculous length of time.

"Damn. I wonder if you could control what someone was doing, like not full possession, but like influence them?" Jack said, sounding interested in finding out, and Harriet wondered if they still might recruit him, after all. It wasn't like their coven ever did anything by the book.

"I'm glad you found out what you are," Harriet said. She couldn't begrudge Cora that much after seeing the sheer joy on Connor's face. She wondered if the rest of the volunteers here were much the same. If they got to test their magic and abilities in ways that their covens or society wouldn't let them outside of the walls of this building. Harriet was more conflicted because she knew the value of knowledge, particularly the satisfaction of it when it had been withheld for so long. However, she knew that agreeing under duress wasn't moral. She could almost see what Cora's vision for this place had been. It would have been lovely, possibly. Just because she trusted Cora's intentions didn't mean she trusted the government's.

"The coast is probably as clear as it's going to get," Dan said, standing from where they'd all been ducked behind the bed. "We need to find Alice and then get out of here as quickly as possible without getting noticed."

Harriet nodded soundly. "Good plan."

"That's your plan?" Connor asked in disbelief. "How the hell did you guys even break in and not get caught?"

"We did get caught," Harriet said, with a grim expression.

"Right," Connor said weakly. "Let's go, then."

*

They made it down two more corridors before Dan pulled the group up short again. Harriet wondered where the hell they were going to hide this time, as the corridor they were in seemed to be for connection purposes only and was narrow and had no rooms along its length. Although the sign above indicated that the girls' and gender neutral rooms were just ahead.

"Oh," Dan said, and he relaxed his stance, just as Petal came bounding around the corner, sans Alice.

"Petal!" Connor cried, kneeling and opening his arms for Petal to run into. She was whining and frantic, twisting in Connor's arms, and headbutting her nose against his sternum.

"Where's Alice?" Connor asked, as Petal whined high, and headbutted him once more before taking a few steps back the way she came, and turned her head, impatiently waiting for them to follow.

161

Harriet didn't want to consider what had happened to Alice that made Petal abandon her to seek help. Thankfully, they didn't have very far to walk before Petal dove sideways into one of the rooms.

Harriet and Connor were the first to enter but couldn't see Alice anywhere. Petal was nosing around the ground where Harriet had to assume Alice had previously been. There was no sign of blood or anything else to indicate Alice had been physically restrained to the room, although Harriet hoped Alice hadn't gone out without Petal.

"She's not here," Connor said. "Where the hell could she have gone?"

Harriet just pursed her lips and shook her head sadly at Connor. "Come on, we're going to find her." The group turned, and Liam made it a single step out the door before he turned straight back around and closed the door quickly but silently.

"Nobody make a sound," Liam breathed.

"*Why?*" Connor mouthed at him.

"*Police,*" Liam mouthed back, and then held up his hand in the shape of a gun to indicate they were armed.

"Everyone hide," Dan whispered.

The group silently made their way back behind the bed, "How are we going to get out?" Harriet asked Liam, her voice barely above a whisper.

"Both sides covered," he said, and it took Harriet a second to realise he meant by opposing sides, police on one side and military guards on the other. Harriet wondered how far Alice had gotten on her own, and prayed she'd made it past the crossfire. Petal was whining softly, and Dan was trying to keep her quiet and still, to no avail.

There was shouting outside, which unfortunately made Petal more anxious and wrigglier in Dan's grasp, but the noise of it drowned out Petal's cries.

"Does Alice have her phone on her?" Connor asked suddenly, having to speak slightly louder to be heard over the noise.

"We all had our phones taken," Harriet said, "Except Dan, but you don't want to use it, trust me."

"Alice didn't have a phone on her when they searched," Dan said.

Connor scoffed, "Alice always has her phone on her. I bet she's still got it. We should—"

The noise of gunfire drowned out what Connor was about to say, and everyone fell silent. Harriet had heard gunfire before, but never so close, and not for a long while. She doubted many of the others had heard it before, especially judging by their shocked expressions.

"I can't believe they're firing," Liam whispered. "They're all going to kill each other."

"We need to tell the police they haven't kidnapped anyone, that they need to stop shooting, they're not criminals, someone is going to get hurt," Jack insisted. Harriet wasn't sure why Jack was looking at her.

"I'm not going out there. I'll get killed," Harriet had avoided it for four hundred and fifty years. She'd like to keep her winning streak going.

"Bullets won't kill you. You're a vampire," Jack said.

Harriet looked at him in disbelief. Harriet wondered if Cora had somehow played their stupid game with Jack as well as Connor, "Yes they will."

Jack, Hayden, and Liam looked confused.

"I still run on blood, even if it's borrowed. A shot to the chest is going to damage my organs. Yeah sure, my deadened skin is slightly tougher, but not bulletproof."

"I thought it was just stakes," Liam insisted.

Harriet nearly rolled her eyes but closed them instead and took a deep breath. She mentally cursed out the younger versions of herself and Cora, insisting on accessible knowledge on magic and still playing that stupid misinformation game.

"A stake to the heart is still going to kill her, just like it would kill a human. Hunters perpetuated it because it meant they could charge a fee for it because it meant they could swoop in and kill vampires because they had the magical weapon that could kill these 'unkillable' creatures. They wouldn't get paid if the townspeople knew a swift blow to the head would do the same trick and they could do it themselves." Connor said.

"Capitalism," Jack scoffed.

Harriet high-fived Connor over his knowledge.

Dan was looking between all of them like they were mad. "This is great, but can we save the history lesson for when people aren't shooting at us?"

Harriet rolled her eyes, "They're not shooting *at us*." But she understood his point. "At any rate, I don't think there's much we can do about the police shooting." Thankfully, since the initial round of shots, there had mostly just been shouting.

"Okay, we still need to find Alice, and then get out," Connor said, tone bitter that he couldn't stop the police and military staff from hurting each other. "I still think we should try messaging Alice to find out where she is."

"Okay," Dan whispered. The voices outside were fading down the corridor towards the far end of the building, retreating off, followed by heavy footsteps advancing after them. Harriet didn't know which group had been at which side.

"We continue looking and you can text her while we do," Dan said, and Connor whipped his phone out and trailed behind the group as they emerged slowly from the room into the corridor.

"Come on. Quietly," Dan said to the group, before taking off at a pace down the corridor. Harriet knew the police and staff were close because she could still hear them shouting further down the corridor.

The group silently crept down the corridor, with Dan and Petal in the lead. Petal was straining against her harness and sniffing at each door they passed.

Suddenly, they heard a noise from one of the rooms several doors down, that sounded automated, "Dude, where are you? We need to get the hell out and we can't find you. Connor."

The group froze as several things happened at once; Petal jolted forward to the same door the noise had come from and started impatiently scratching at the wooden frame. Harriet and Connor looked at each other wide eyed as they realised that Alice must have an automated voice to read out her texts for her, and the voices down the end of the corridor paused, before once loudly said, "You lot, check back down there."

"Dammit," Connor said. Thankfully, Dan snapped into action and dragged Connor and Harriet by the arms to the door. He let go to open the door and Petal barged in ahead of them. The coven didn't seem to freeze either and were right behind them as they pushed everyone in the room from behind and closed the door, uncaring how loud the noise was.

Alice was sat behind the bed, hugging Petal. "I have never been so relieved to feel your auras before," she said in the group's general direction. "And I'm so relieved to have you back," Alice said to Petal, "it's like losing your sight all over again, I knew I should have brought my stick."

The voices outside were getting closer and Harriet could hear them starting to kick doors in. She shared a worried glance with Dan. They'd never survive the drop out the window. They were three floors up and it was a solid concrete landing.

"So how are we getting out?" Alice asked.

Dan frowned, "I don't know that we are."

Alice nodded, "The police are here though, right? That's what all the shouting and that was about, so they'll get us out, right?"

Dan winced, "Technically, Connor and Jack are the only ones who got kidnapped, and even Jack is arguable, considering we all stowed away on the van to get inside the building. We could get done for trespassing, and Harriet and Connor might yet get done for breaking and entering into Mr Jones' place. At any rate, Wellard could very well do us for withholding information, and at a stretch, obstruction of justice, depending what mood he's in when he finds us."

Harriet let Dan's words wash over her as she tried to mentally bring up the map in her head. She and Dan had come up the stairs on the far side of the building, back past the boys' rooms and the rec centre, but there was another stairwell in the middle of the building. They'd passed it when they followed Petal. If they could get back to that staircase, they might make it back down to the ground floor and somehow out.

They just needed a way to get past whoever was breaking down the doors. Harriet figured they hadn't got many more doors left before finding them, and they were going to have to think fast.

Harriet could have screamed from frustration. How the hell did they end up in this situation? She had wanted a quiet year to get through her dissertation, and maybe try and work out what she wanted to do for the rest of her life. She was sick of people trying to kidnap and kill her friends. She just wanted to go back to quiet nights in the library, where the most dangerous adventure ended in getting reprimanded by the university board or Sabina, who was used to their antics, not getting shot at. Harriet ground her teeth together in anger. It was time to bite back. Metaphorically, of course.

"I think I know how we can get to the ground floor," Harriet said to Dan. "I don't know how we get out from there, though."

"My pack got here after the police, so they can't get through the barricade, but I can tell them to have the car on standby," Dan said. "How do we get down there?"

"We passed a stairwell on the way here," Harriet rushed. Three more doors had been broken down and rooms ransacked. "I'm going to distract them, while one person makes a break for the stairs and everyone else is gonna need to be shrunken back down and carried."

Dan nodded. "And how are you going to distract them?"

"I'm going to run at them."

Even Dan looked at her like that was a bad idea.

"Are you a moron?" Connor said angrily. "You know the bullets can hurt you."

"They won't fire. They'll just arrest me, probably," Harriet said. As long as she didn't startle them too much or look like she was going to drink their blood as she ran at them. This was a terrible idea.

"Connor, try your semi-possession thing. Maybe you could magic them into dropping their guns," Jack said.

"I don't even know if that's something I can do. Why don't you shrink everyone? At least they might not find us when they check the room," Connor shot back.

"No," Alice said with a tone of finality. "I've had enough. No untried demon magic, no running at men with guns and certainly no shrinking again. Three times in quick succession cannot be good for the skeletal structure."

Even the coven looked like they agreed with that last bit. "Magic has consequences." Alice continued. "I'm going." When everyone started to protest, Alice gave them a filthy look, and said, "Trust me, I know what I'm doing."

Harriet would have protested, but the door flew open and sent her and Dan who were leaning on it, flying onto the floor. Apparently arguing loudly amongst yourselves was the quickest way to get caught.

"Everyone stay where they are. We're not going to hurt you," the police said, waving their guns in an incredibly contrary manner.

Harriet watched as everyone bar Alice joined her and Dan on the floor.

"Ma'am, please sit on the floor until we've searched the rest of this room."

"How many are there?" Alice asked Dan, which seemed to confuse the police officer further.

"Ma'am." He jostled his gun, as if to draw her attention towards it, "Please sit on the ground with the rest of your group."

"Two here, four further down the corridor," Dan said.

"Hey, keep quiet," The officer said to Dan. "Ma'am, please could you-urk." The officers voice cut off as he appeared to choke on air. The second officer, who'd started searching the room appeared to be having a similar problem. Harriet saw Dan's head tilted as if he were listening to the corridor outside, possibly where the same thing was also happening. Suddenly, the two men dropped to the ground and even Harriet heard the four other thuds from the corridor. Alice also dropped with them.

"Holy shit!" Jack said.

Harriet and Dan checked Alice's pulse point and tried to gently shake her awake, respectively. Alice roused quickly.

"Did it work?" she asked.

"Are they dead?" Connor asked, none too gently kicking the officer's side; the one who'd pointed his gun at Alice and Dan.

Liam shook his head. He was taking the other officer's pulse. "Unconscious."

"Why didn't you do that before?" Jack asked. "That was epic."

"It takes a lot of energy. It's more of a last resort. Besides, I've never tried it on so many before. I wasn't sure exactly what was going to happen. I've been reading up on how fainting works in the hope that I would be able to induce it with magic."

"Right. Let's go before any more come back," Harriet said, and gestured for Dan to carry Alice. Harriet stuck her head out the door and when no one else came down the corridor, she gestured for them all to run as fast as possible to the ground floor.

"Connor," Dan huffed, still managing to keep pace with the rest of them, despite the fact he was carrying Alice. "Call Madison. No doubt she will have tagged along. Tell her to get the pack ready for a quick retreat from the back of the building."

Connor nodded and grabbed his phone from his pocket, heavily pressing on the buttons as he tried not to let his stride falter.

Harriet was in slight disbelief. They were actually going to make it out.

*

Harriet had thought her earlier optimism was going to be the preclude to another hurdle. Thankfully, Dan insisted on using the lift so they didn't meet anyone in the stairwell and they reached the ground floor in under a minute.

The group had made it to the back of the building, back into the warehouse that they initially been driven into. They'd only come across a few policemen standing guard, but the coven had knocked them unconscious. Not using Alice's spell, because they didn't know how she'd done it. They'd just punched the officers in the face and hoped for the best.

When they reached the warehouse doors, a large van pulled up with a manically grinning Madison behind the wheel. Behind her was the remains of the police tape cordoning off the area, and several officers were running towards the van.

"Get in, losers," she grinned. Dan rolled his eyes, and Harriet realised the dramatics were inherited. Connor hoped in the front with her and gave her a high five.

"Let's get back to normality," Dan said, as he closed the van door behind them, the van already having started speeding off.

Harriet couldn't agree more.

Chapter Twenty-Five

Obviously, there had been a conversation with the police where they'd all been called in to give statements. However, Wellard had seemed embarrassed enough about the whole ordeal, and had clearly been reprimanded for going in all guns blazing, because he hadn't wanted to admit a group of uni students, and a coven had beaten him to it. So, no formal charges were pressed.

He did, however, give all of them his best withering look.

Cora had not been brought up during the interview with the police and so Harriet had come to the relieved conclusion that nobody had mentioned it to them. Harriet had been forced to fill them all in on what happened as Dan asked her loudly in front of everyone. She'd told them what Cora had done, and what she'd said to Harriet. Harriet then told them that she had let Cora go, to which there had been mixed responses, but Harriet had impressed upon them the need to keep it quiet in front of the police. Apparently, they had all had the wherewithal to listen to her.

Harriet had received a letter off Cora a couple of weeks after the facility had been shut down. It *had* been shut down, despite a ruling that nothing illegal had gone on and the government breathed a sigh of relief and pointed the finger at one of the men who had been closely working with Cora. As Cora had predicted, public outrage managed to close the doors quicker than any jury could have. Cora thankfully did not point this out in her letter. All it said was that she had settled into her new town, and that she hoped she would see Harriet soon. It was signed Evelyn, but Harriet recognised the writing. Harriet wondered why Cora had chosen to go back to her birth name. She hadn't seemed too sad to say goodbye to it the first time they'd moved towns, although they'd both grown attached to the names Harriet and Cora and decided to keep them sometime after the mid-19th century. Harriet couldn't even remember what her first name had originally been now.

She hadn't written back to Cora, Evelyn, and she probably wouldn't for a while; she had mostly forgiven Cora for what she had done. It had all been in the pursuit of knowledge, and Harriet would be a hypocrite not to forgive her, having taught her that knowledge should be held above all else, and of course that Harriet had done some definitively illegal things herself, she should definitely strive to become a better role model.

Vampires could afford to hold grudges, though, and there were definitely simpler ways Cora could have avoided this, mainly be coming to talk to Harriet. So, Harriet decided to let her stew for a while. Cora wouldn't be able to come back for a few years anyway, just in case.

Although Harriet was softening to her cause somewhat when she heard the tales from the 'kidnapped' girls, and they had confirmed Cora's story. The girls had been well treated and had been happy. Most of their covens were apologetic, having heard that their actions had driven their daughters and granddaughters to be taken into a 'lab', and they had come begging for the girls to come back to the safety of their covens.

Thankfully, most of the girls had not followed Ms Pickett's actions, and had disavowed their covens and created their own. Headed by Alice. Harriet wasn't quite sure how it worked, as Alice was still, nominally at least, in her previous coven. Harriet had asked Alice how she persuaded the girls to start their own coven with her heading, as she'd only been in the facility for a matter of hours. Alice had told her it was because her reputation for rebelling from within her own coven had gotten around from Lucy. Personally, Harriet thought she was just bossy, and the other girls hadn't minded. It seemed to work, at any rate, and Ms Pickett had let the girls stay at her house and use it as a coven home, having finally disavowed her own coven.

Jack, Liam, and Hayden were still in their own coven, although they made frequent trips round to Pickett's house and Alice had mentioned setting up a network of covens to freely share information. Harriet assumed it was going well, as the boys' coven seemed to be out searching for more male witches, they also seemed to be blowing things up on a less regular schedule, although Harriet figured that was more likely due to them being busy, as opposed to streamlining their potion making skills.

Jack mentioned that they had asked Connor to join their coven. He wouldn't tell Harriet exactly what Connor said, but when Harriet broke down and just plain asked Connor, he just shook his head, and said he'd declined, although they were trying to help him discover what exactly being half-demon meant.

They hadn't discovered anything yet, but Connor remained hopeful, "It took me twenty years to discover what I am. I can wait a little longer to work out what it means."

The boys also promised to keep an eye out for any other half-demons in their search for male witches, although again, they hadn't turned up anything yet.

Although Harriet doubted that they would, even Sabina hadn't heard of half-demons before, although she had seemed intrigued and requested a meeting with Connor when she'd found out. Connor had his first meeting with the dean, and finally learnt why Harriet had laughed at him when they'd last discussed Sabina. He came out of the meeting looking as shocked and confused as anyone would after an eight-year-old looking woman inquired about your late mother's demonic activity.

Connor grumbled at her about it, but it was worth it to see the dawning realisation on his face when he had entered Sabina's office.

"I feel sorry for Sabina," Dan said, after Connor finished his current rant. They were back at the coffee shop, but Dan was sat with them in the booth.

"What?" Connor asked, betrayed.

Harriet raised an eyebrow and Dan smirked. "He's been compiling a list of questions for her ever since. I think he's reached three pages now."

Connor elbowed Dan as Harriet snorted.

"Shouldn't you be working?" Connor asked, pointedly not looking at Dan.

Dan rolled his eyes and stood back up, walking back over to where his packmate, Ellie, was manning the counter. She winked conspicuously at Connor, and loudly proclaimed, "Don't worry Dan, I'm sure you can buy his affections back with brownies."

To which Dan huffed, and then pretended to deal with stock in the back, leaving the rest of them laughing.

It was a relatively new thing between Connor and Dan, having happened not long after they'd 'rescued' Connor from the lab. Harriet and Connor had been at the coffee shop and Harriet had asked Connor how he was feeling, and Connor had said, "Well, after my near-death experience—"

"Don't be dramatic. You were in nicer digs than I am now," Harriet had replied. Connor had been teasing the lot of them mercilessly about their 'heroic' rescue.

"After my near-death experience, I have learned the value of going after what I want."

Harriet had asked him what that was, and Connor's eyes had flickered over to Dan. Which Harriet thought was sweet, until Connor's eyes had slid downwards, and then Harriet pretended to throw up her cup of blood, which caused the sleep deprived witch opposite them to look briefly alarmed. In the following conversation about whether or not Connor leering at Dan was romantic or not, Harriet and Connor had forgotten about werewolf hearing until Dan came over and asked if they would stop talking because Ellie was live texting their conversation back to the rest of his pack.

Harriet figured it all worked out in the end.

"How's your dissertation coming along?" Connor asked, and Harriet flicked back to the present conversation.

"Barely," Harriet complained. She had mostly succeeded, especially now Mr Jones had been reinstated back. Harriet hadn't thought he was going to stick around once the police had cleared him. Even though she'd had a full three months in which no one was trying to kidnap or kill her friends to get on with university work, she was still slightly behind. Simon had restarted the counter on when she was next going to get in trouble though. He and Liam had formed an unholy alliance, and now every witch, werewolf and vampire was in on the betting.

"Pickett has actually been properly nice to me since the whole lab thing, and now it's driving all the witches in my class crazy on how I became her favourite," Connor seemed unduly delighted at the news.

Harriet laughed. "I know. I passed her the other day and she smiled at me."

"That's only because you're the department's newest researcher," Connor said slyly.

"How did you know?" Harriet asked. She'd only said yes to Sabina yesterday.

"Why didn't you tell me? I thought you didn't want to go into academia. Was it Pickett's smile? Did it shock you into saying yes?" Connor leaned forward in his seat eagerly.

Harriet shook her head, "No, I just—I don't know. I didn't want to become a stuffy academic for all eternity, but instead I've ended up a perpetual student. Figured it's time to actually figure out what I want to do, and if in another four hundred years I decide it's time for a change of scenery, then so be it."

Simon had been thrilled she was joining the staff side of the university and had promised to fill her in on all of the gossip. Harriet figured *Evelyn* would be pleased at the news when she finally got around to sending her reply, especially as she had decided her research focus was going to be on interviewing supernaturals and trying to encourage more open communication, the sharing of knowledge.

"Good for you," Connor grinned, "And don't worry, I bet there's loads more crazy stuff going on in the staff room. Shady government organisations and shootings were just the tip of the iceberg."

Harriet laughed. "As long as you promise to keep breaking and entering with me."

Connor grinned, and although she didn't have werewolf hearing, she was pretty sure she could hear Dan's long-suffering sigh from here.

It was going to be an eventful next century at least.